Penguin Books
Sunset at Blandings

Pelham Grenville Wodehouse was born in Guildford,
the son of a civil servant, and educated at Dulwich College. He
spent a brief period working for the Hong Kong and Shanghai
Bank before abandoning finance for writing, earning a living by
journalism and selling stories to magazines.

An enormously popular and prolific writer, he produced
about a hundred books, and was probably best known for
creating Jeeves, the ever resourceful 'gentleman's personal
gentleman', and the good-hearted young blunderer Bertie
Wooster. However, Wodehouse created many other comic
figures, perhaps most notably the inhabitants of, and regular
visitors to, Blandings Castle and its environs. He wrote the
many Blandings stories over the course of more than sixty
years; the first, *Something Fresh*, appeared in 1915, while at the
time of his death he was working on the posthumously
published *Sunset at Blandings*. He was part-author and writer
of fifteen straight plays and of 250 lyrics for some thirty
musical comedies. *The Times* hailed him as a 'comic genius
recognized in his lifetime as a classic and an old master of
farce'.

P. G. Wodehouse said, 'I believe there are two ways of
writing novels. One is mine, making a sort of musical comedy
without music and ignoring real life altogether; the other is
going right deep down into life and not caring a damn.'

Wodehouse married in 1914 and took American citizenship
in 1955. He was created a Knight of the British Empire in the
1975 New Year's Honours List. In a BBC interview he said that
he had no ambitions left now that he had been knighted and
there was a waxwork of him in Madame Tussaud's. He died on
St Valentine's Day, 1975, at the age of ninety-three.

About the Editors

Richard Usborne joined an advertising agency after Oxford before becoming a writer and journalist. He was, for three years, assistant editor of *Strand* magazine. In 1953 he wrote *Clubland Heroes*, a review of the works of Sapper, Buchan and Dornford Yates. Wodehouse enjoyed it so much that he asked for Usborne to write the book published as *Wodehouse at Work*. He has subsequently edited several Wodehouse collections, as well as serializing a number of Wodehouse stories for radio.

Norman Murphy began his investigations into the factual origins of Wodehouse's novels in 1972, as an army officer serving in Whitehall. His book, *In Search of Blandings*, was first published in 1981.

Tony Ring has already published six of the planned eight volumes in the *Millennium Wodehouse Concordance*, which will survey all Wodehouse's fiction when complete. His *You Simply Hit Them With An Axe* (1995) concerned Wodehouse's tax problems.

P. G. Wodehouse published and forthcoming in Penguin

P. G. Wodehouse

Sunset
at
Blandings

with *Notes and Appendices by*
Richard Usborne

Revised and Updated by
N. T. P. Murphy and Tony Ring

Foreword by
Douglas Adams

PENGUIN BOOKS

PENGUIN BOOKS

Published by the Penguin Group
Penguin Books Ltd, 27 Wrights Lane, London w8 5 tz, England
Penguin Putnam Inc., 375 Hudson Street, New York, New York 10014, USA
Penguin Books Australia Ltd, Ringwood, Victoria, Australia
Penguin Books Canada Ltd, 10 Alcorn Avenue, Toronto, Ontario, Canada m4v 3b2
Penguin Books (NZ) Ltd, Private Bag 102902, NSMC, Auckland, New Zealand

Penguin Books Ltd, Registered Offices: Harmondsworth, Middlesex, England

First published in Great Britain by Chatto & Windus 1977
Published in Penguin Books 1990
This revised and amended edition published 2000
10 9 8 7 6 5 4 3 2 1

Set in 9/11pt Monotype Trump
Typeset by Rowland Phototypesetting Ltd,
Bury St Edmunds, Suffolk
Printed in England by Clays Ltd, St Ives plc

Contents

BLANDINGS
CASTLE
SHROPSHIRE

To SHREWSBURY

The WREKIN

TRIBUTARY OF
RIVER SEVERN

RIVER
SEVERN

SUNNYBRAE

BLANDINGS PARVA

MAIN GATES
AND
LODGES

WEST WOOD

YEW ALLEY

GAMEKEEPER'S
COTTAGE

PADDOCK

PADDOCK

OLD PIG-STY
AND PADDOCK

TRIBUTARY OF
RIVER SEVERN

17 18 19 20 21 22 23 24 25 26 27 28 29

A B C D E F G H J K L M N P Q R S T U V W X Y

To SHREWSBURY
MARKET BLANDINGS
MUCH MATCHINGHAM
SAW MILL
MATCHINGHAM HALL
SECOND PIG-STY
GREEN HOUSE
PIG-MAN'S COTTAGE
ESTATE WORKERS COTTAGES
BOTTLING SHED
KITCHEN GARDENS
FACTOR'S HOUSE
POND
STABLES GARAGES, STORES, &c.
ESTATE OFFICE
BOWLING GREEN· CROQUET LAWN
TENNIS COURTS
ROSE GARDEN
SUMMER HOUSE
BATHING HUT
BOAT HOUSE

IONICUS 1977

Foreword

This is P. G. Wodehouse's last – and unfinished – book. It is unfinished not just in the sense that it suddenly, heartbreakingly for those of us who love this man and his work, stops in mid-flow, but in the more important sense that the text up to that point is also unfinished. A first draft for Wodehouse was a question of getting the essential ingredients of a story organized – its plot structure, its characters, their comings and goings, the mountains they climb and the cliffs they fall off. It is the next stage of writing – the relentless revising, refining and polishing – that turned his works into the marvels of language we know and love. When he was writing a book he used to pin the pages in undulating waves around the wall of his workroom. Pages he felt were working well would be pinned up high and those that still needed work would be lower down the wall. His aim was to get the entire manuscript up to the picture rail before he handed it in.

Much of *Sunset at Blandings* would probably still have been obscured by the chair backs. It was a work in progress. Many of the lines in it are just placeholders for what would come in later revisions – the dazzling images and conceits that would send the pages shooting up the walls.

Will you, anyway, find much evidence of the great genius of Wodehouse here? Well, to be honest, no. Not just because it is an unfinished work in progress, but also because at the time of writing he was what can only be described as ninety-three. At that age I think you are entitled to have your best work behind you. In a way,

Wodehouse was condemned by his extreme longevity (he was born the year before Darwin died and was still working well after the Beatles had split up) to end up playing Pierre Menard to his own Cervantes. (I'm not going to unravel that for you. If you don't know what I'm talking about, you should read Jorge Luis Borges' short story 'Pierre Menard, Author of Quixote'. It's only six pages long and you'll be wanting to drop me a postcard to thank me for pointing it out to you.) But you will want to read *Sunset* for completeness, and for that sense you get, from its very unfinishedness, of being suddenly and unexpectedly close to a Master actually at work – a bit like seeing paint pots and scaffolding being carried in and out of the Sistine Chapel.

Master? Great genius? Oh yes. One of the most blissful joys of the English language is the fact that one of its greatest practitioners ever, one of the guys on the very top table of all, was a jokesmith. Though maybe it shouldn't be that big a surprise. Who else would be up there? Austen, of course, Dickens and Chaucer. The only one who couldn't make a joke to save his life would be Shakespeare.

Oh come on, let's be frank and fearless for a moment. There's nothing worse than watching a certain kind of English actor valiantly trying to ham it up as, for instance, Dogberry in *Much Ado*. It's desperate stuff. We even draw a veil over the whole buttock-clenching business by calling the comic device he employs in that instance 'malapropism' – after Sheridan's character Mrs Malaprop who does exactly the same thing, only funny, in *The Rivals*. And it's no good saying it's something to do with the fact that Shakespeare was writing in the sixteenth century. What difference does that make? Chaucer had no difficulty being as funny as hell way back in the fourteenth century when the spelling was even worse.

Maybe it's because our greatest writing genius was

incapable of being funny that we have decided that being funny doesn't count. Which is tough on Wodehouse (as if he could have cared less) because his entire genius was for being funny, and being funny in such a sublime way as to put mere poetry in the shade. The precision with which he plays upon every aspect of a word's character simultaneously – its meaning, timbre, rhythm, the range of its idiomatic connections and flavours – would make Keats whistle. Keats would have been proud to have written 'the smile vanished from his face like breath off a razor-blade', or of Honoria Glossop's laugh that it sounded like 'cavalry on a tin bridge'. Speaking of which, Shakespeare, when he wrote that a man 'may smile, and smile, and be a villain' might have been at least as impressed by, 'Many a man may look respectable, and yet be able to hide at will behind a spiral staircase.'

What Wodehouse writes is pure word music. It matters not one whit that he writes endless variations on a theme of pig kidnappings, lofty butlers and ludicrous impostures. He is the greatest *musician* of the English language and exploring variations of familiar material is what musicians do all day. In fact, what it's *about* seems to me to be wonderfully irrelevant. Beauty doesn't have to be *about* anything. What's a vase about? What's a sunset or a flower about? What, for that matter, is Mozart's Twenty-third Piano Concerto *about*? It is said that all art tends towards the condition of music, and music isn't *about* anything – unless it's not very good music. Film music is about something. The Dam Busters' March is about something. A Bach fugue, on the other hand, is pure form, beauty and playfulness, and I'm not sure that very much, in terms of human art and achievement, lies beyond a Bach fugue. Maybe the quantum electrodynamic theory of light. Maybe 'Uncle Fred Flits By'. I don't know.

Evelyn Waugh, I think, compared Wodehouse's world to a pre-fall Eden, and it's true that, in Blandings, Plum –

if I may call him that – has managed to create and sustain an entirely innocent and benign Paradise, a task which, we may recall, famously defeated Milton, who was probably trying too hard. Like Milton, Wodehouse reaches outside his Paradise for the metaphors that will make it real for his readers. But where Milton reaches, rather confusingly, into the world of classical gods and heroes for his images (like a TV writer who only draws his references from other TV shows), Wodehouse is vividly real. 'She was standing scrutinizing the safe, and heaving gently like a Welsh rarebit about to come to the height of its fever.' 'The Duke's moustache was rising and falling like seaweed on an ebb-tide.' When it comes to making metaphors (well, all right, similes if you insist) don't mess with the Master. Of course, Wodehouse never burdened himself with the task of justifying the ways of God to Man, but only of making Man, for a few hours at a time, inextinguishably happy.

Wodehouse better than Milton? Well, of course it's an absurd comparison, but I know which one I'd keep in the balloon, and not just for his company, but for his art.

We Wodehouse fans are very fond of phoning each other up with new discoveries. But we may do the great man a disservice when we pull out our favourite quotes in public, like, 'Ice formed on the butler's upper slopes', or 'like so many substantial Americans, he had married young and kept on marrying, springing from blonde to blonde like the chamois of the Alps leaping from crag to crag' or (here I go again) my current favourite, 'He spun round with a sort of guilty bound, like an adagio dancer surprised while watering the cat's milk', because, irreducibly wonderful though they are, by themselves they are a little like stuffed fish on a mantelpiece. You need to see them in action to get the full effect. There is not much in Freddie Threepwood's isolated line, 'I have here in this sack a few simple rats' to tell you that when you read it in context you are at the pinnacle of one of the most sublime moments in all English literature.

Shakespeare? Milton? Keats? How can I possibly mention the author of *Pearls, Girls and Monty Bodkin* and *Pigs Have Wings* in the same breath as these men? He's just not serious!

He doesn't need to be serious. He's better than that. He's up in the stratosphere of what the human mind can do, above tragedy and strenuous thought, where you will find Bach, Mozart, Einstein, Feynman and Louis Armstrong, in the realms of pure, creative playfulness.

DOUGLAS ADAMS

Introduction

Sunset at Blandings is the incomplete eleventh and last novel to be set at Blandings Castle, and consists of the draft first sixteen chapters of a book that was planned to have twenty-two. They were written by a great humorist at the age of ninety-three whose previous novel, *Aunts Aren't Gentlemen*, had been a number one bestseller in England in 1974.

These sixteen chapters, typed out on Wodehouse's favourite old 1927 Royal, their pages numbered 1–90, were in the hospital with him when he died on 14 February 1975. In addition, 183 pages of notes and drafts for this novel were found after his death, thirty-three of them in the hospital, 150 of them from among the papers in his study at home.

Among the pages of notes and drafts which were found with Plum was a Scenario, dated 19 January 1975, which summarized the plot of the remaining six chapters as he saw them at that time. That is not to say the final plot would have followed those guidelines, for they left unanswered questions, merely that they represented the best out-turn the author had selected to date.

The Scenario may be found in full on pages 118 to 123, in two forms. On the left-hand page is a facsimile of his typed notes with manuscript alterations, while on the right-hand page, for clarity, the notes have been typeset.

Many of the other pages of notes had clearly been superseded as Wodehouse had worked on the first draft of the novel. But one problem he did not seem to have solved fully was precisely how Florence Moresby's second husband, Kevin, fitted in. As a further example of how Wodehouse worked, and to allow readers' imaginations to develop their own ideas, further pages of manuscript notes have been included at pages 124 to 128 with the typed transcription opposite.

When *Sunset at Blandings* was first published by Chatto & Windus in 1977, and in its subsequent appearance as a Penguin, it was accompanied by a considerably more extensive selection of Wodehouse's working notes, analysed in some detail by Richard Usborne. In preparing this edition it was concluded that, twenty-five years after Wodehouse's death, it was of lesser importance to include material that had no bearing on the latest version of the Scenario as the author saw it. Nevertheless, the part of Richard Usborne's summary relating to how Wodehouse might have resolved the remaining problems has been included.

Usborne had also prepared a number of footnotes to the text of the first sixteen chapters, and these have been revised and updated. In some cases they have been shortened and depersonalized, whilst several new footnotes have been added.

Sunset at Blandings is one of a small handful of books by Wodehouse which one should not recommend as an introduction to this great author's works. As the given text merely represents a first draft, it does not have the polish which would have been added by the author in the next stage of his writing: the introduction of new 'nifties', the original similes or applied misquotations of which Evelyn Waugh spoke so highly. He would have found ways of lengthening some of his humorous scenes, and would have tightened up some of the inconsistencies identified in the footnotes. No, this is not the book for a Wodehouse novice. It is for the more experienced reader, already familiar with a number of volumes in the Blandings series.

Finally, for those readers who have persevered this far, a few words about the title. It was not one selected by Wodehouse himself. He had jotted down fifteen ideas:

All's Well at Blandings	*Leave it to Galahad*	*The Helping Hand of Galahad*
Blandings Castle Fills Up	*Life with Galahad*	*The Weird Old Buster*
Gally in Charge	*Lord Emsworth Entertains*	*Trouble at Blandings Castle*
Gally Takes Charge	*Love at the Castle*	*Unrest at Blandings Castle*
Gally to the Rescue	*Rely on Gally*	*Women are Peculiar*

The title *Sunset at Blandings* was suggested by Chatto & Windus, and seems endearingly appropriate.

TONY RING

I

Sir James Piper, England's[1] Chancellor of the Exchequer, sat in his London study staring before him with what are usually called unseeing eyes and snorting every now and then like somebody bursting a series of small paper bags. Sherlock Holmes, had he seen him, would have deduced instantly that he was not in a good temper.

'Elementary, my dear Watson,' he would have said. 'Those snorts tell the story.'

And Claude Duff, Sir James's junior secretary, who had been intending to ask him if he could have the day off to go and see his aunt at Eastbourne, heard these snorts and changed his mind. He was a nervous young man.

Holmes would have been right. Sir James had been in the worst of humours ever since his sister Brenda had told him that he was to go to Blandings Castle, the Shropshire seat of Clarence, Earl of Emsworth, when he had been planning a fishing holiday in Scotland. And what was worse, he had got to take a girl with him and deliver her to the custody of Lord Emsworth's sister Florence.[2] He disliked modern girls. They were jumpy. They wriggled and giggled. They had no conversation. A long motor journey beside one of them, having to stare at Sergeant Murchison's back all the way, would test him sorely, and not for the first time he found himself wishing that he had a stronger will or, alternatively, that Brenda had a weaker one. Lord Emsworth, that vague and dreamy peer, would have told him that he knew just how he felt. He, too, was a great sufferer from the tyranny of sisters, of whom he had sufficient to equip half a dozen earls.

It was Brenda who had forced James into politics when a distant relative had left him all that money in her will. He had been at the time a happy young lad-about-town wanting nothing but to remain a happy young lad-about-town, but Brenda was adamant. It is said that there is a woman behind every successful man, and never had the statement been proved more remarkably than in the case of young Jimmy Piper.

Today he thoroughly enjoyed politics and the eminence to which he had risen, and he knew that he would never have done it without her behind him with a spiked stick. Often in the early days he had wanted to give the whole thing up – he could still recall with a shudder what a priceless ass he had felt when making his first appearance before the electors of Pudbury-in-the-Vale – but Brenda would have none of it. He supposed he ought to feel grateful to her, and as a rule he did, but when she suddenly produced girls like rabbits out of a hat, gratitude turned to sullen wrath and he felt justified in snorting with even more vehemence.

Brenda came in as he increased the voltage of his eleventh snort, a formidable figure, formidably dressed. Had she been weaker, she might have shown sympathy for the stricken man, but her deportment and words were those of a strong-minded governess who believed in standing no nonsense from a fractious child.

'Oh, really, James, must you make such a crisis of it? You are behaving like an aristocrat of the French Revolution waiting for the tumbril. I'd like to be coming with you, but I can't get away for a day or two. I have that committee meeting.'

If Sir James had been a man of greater mettle, a twelfth snort might have escaped him. As it was, he merely said:

'Who is this girl I'm taking to the castle?'

'Surely I told you?'

'You may have done. I've forgotten.'

'Florence's stepdaughter Victoria. Florence most unwisely let her come to London to study Art, and she has apparently got involved with an impossible young man. Naturally Florence wants her where she can keep an eye on her.'[3]

She had more to say, but at this point a knock on the door interrupted her. There entered a soberly dressed man who gave the impression of having been carved out of some durable kind of wood by a sculptor who had received his tuition from an inefficient tutor. This was Sergeant E. B. Murchison, the detective appointed by the special branch of Scotland Yard to accompany Sir James wherever he went and see to it that he came to no harm from the terror by night and the arrow that flieth by day. He said:

'The car is at the door, Sir James.'[4]

Sir James made no reply, and Brenda answered for him with a gracious 'Thank you, Sergeant'. He withdrew, and Sir James looked after him in a manner most unsuitable towards an honest helper who was prepared, if necessary, to die in his defence.

'God, how I hate that man,' he muttered.

It was the sort of remark which called out all the governess in Brenda. Her face, always on the stony side, grew stonier. It was as though Sir James had kicked the furniture or refused to eat his rice pudding.

'Don't be childish, James.'

'Who's being childish?'

'You're being childish. You have no reason whatever to dislike Sergeant Murchison.'

'Haven't I? How would you like being followed around wherever you go? How would you enjoy being dogged from morning to night by a man who makes you feel as if you were someone wanted by the police because they think you may be able to assist them in their enquiries? I expect daily, when I take a bath, to find Murchison nestling in the soap dish.'

Miss Piper had no patience with these tantrums.

'My dear James, a man in your position has to have protection.'

'Why? What's he supposed to be protecting me *from*? Is Blandings Castle the den of the Secret Nine? Is Emsworth a modern Macbeth? Is he going to creep into my room at night with a dagger? And if he does, how can that blasted Murchison protect me? How can he stop anyone assassinating me if he's snoring his repulsive head off a quarter of a mile away? Or will he be sleeping on the mat outside my door? I don't know what you're laughing at,' said Sir James with *hauteur*, for Brenda's face had softened into an amused smile.

'I was picturing Lord Emsworth as a modern Macbeth.'

Sir James had thought of something else to complain about.

'Shall I be plunging into the middle of a large party? Public dinners are bad enough, but big country house parties are worse. I always used to hate them, even as a young man.'

'Of course it won't be a large party. Just Florence and her sister Diana Phipps.[5] What on earth's the matter, James?' said Brenda petulantly, for Sir James had leaped like one of the trout he was so fond of catching. His eyes were gleaming with a strange light and he had to gulp before he could speak.

'Nothing's the matter.'

'You jumped.'

'You surprised me, saying that Diana Phipps was at Blandings. I thought she lived in East Africa.'

'You know her?'

'I used to know her ages ago. Before,' said Sir James, and he spoke bitterly, 'she chucked herself away on that ass Rollo[6] Phipps.'

'I always heard he was very attractive.'

'If you call looking like a film star attractive. Not a brain in his head. Spent all his time shooting big game. My God!' said Sir James with sudden alarm, 'There's no danger of him being at Blandings?'

'Not unless he is haunting the castle. He was killed by a lion years ago.'

'And nobody told me!'

'Why should anyone tell you?'

'Because . . . because I would have liked to extend my sympathy to Diana.'

One of the gifts which go to make up the type of superwomen to whom Brenda belonged is the ability to read faces. Brenda had it in full measure, especially where her brother was concerned.

'James!' Her voice was at its keenest. 'Were you in love with her?'

It might have been supposed that a man of Sir James's long experience as a Cabinet minister would have replied 'I must have notice of that question', but excitement precluded caution. His mind was in a ferment and had flitted back to the days before he had come into all that money and gone into politics, the days when he had been plain Jimmy Piper, longing to make an impression on lovely Diana Threepwood but always tongue-tied, always elbowed to one side by the fellows with the gift of the gab. It was only later, gradually rising on stepping-stones of his dead self to higher things, that he had acquired the politician's ability to use a great many words when saying nothing.

'Of course I was in love with her,' he replied with defiance. 'We were all in love with her. And she went and threw herself away on Rollo Phipps.'

'Well, he's dead now.'

'Yes, that's something.'

'And she's at Blandings.'

'Yes.'

'And you're going to Blandings.'

'Yes.'

'You're probably glad of it now.'

'Yes.'

'You intend to ask her to marry you?'

'Yes.'

'It would be an excellent thing for both of you.'

'Yes.'

'But there is one thing I must warn you about. I have never met Diana, but if she is anything like the other Threepwood girls, she abominates weakness.'[7]

'I'm not weak.'

'You're shy, which can quite easily give that impression. So when you propose, don't stammer and yammer. Be firm. Dominate her. Otherwise she won't look at you.'

'I'll remember.'

'Mind you do. Those girls abominate weakness.'

'You said that before.'

'And I say it again. Look at Florence and her husband.'

'I always thought Underwood was one of those steel and iron American millionaires.'

'Her second husband. Underwood died, and she married a man who couldn't say Bo to a goose.'

'Very rude of him if he did, unless he knew the goose very well.'

'That's why Florence and her husband are separated.'[8]

'They are, are they?'

'He's weak. You wouldn't think it to look at him, because he's one of those extraordinary virile men in appearance. If you can imagine a Greek god with a small clipped moustache . . . You had better be starting, James. You heard Sergeant Murchison say the car was waiting.'

'Let it wait. You don't know who else will be at Blandings, do you?'

'No, Florence didn't say.'

'I was wondering if Gally would be there.'

'Who?'

'Galahad Threepwood.'

'I sincerely hope not,' said Brenda.

Like the majority of his sisters, she thoroughly disapproved of Lord Emsworth's younger brother.

'Do you see anything of Galahad Threepwood nowadays?' she asked suspiciously.

'Haven't seen him for years. We were great friends in the old days.'

The snort which proceeded from Brenda might not have been a snort of the calibre of those which her brother had emitted, but it was definitely a sniff. The subject of the old days was one normally avoided by both of them – on his part from caution, on hers because the mere thought of those days revolted her. She preferred not to be reminded that there had been a time, before she took charge of him, when James had moved in a most undesirable circle – a member in fact of the Pelican Club[9] to which Galahad Threepwood had belonged.

'I believe he has a prison record,' she said.

Sir James hastened to correct this hasty statement.

'No, he was always given the option of a fine.'

'You are keeping the car waiting,' said Brenda coldly.

2

Jno Robinson's taxi,[10] which meets all the trains at
Market Blandings, drew up with a screeching of brakes
at the great door of Blandings Castle, and a dapper little
man of the type one automatically associates in one's
mind with white bowler hats and race glasses bumping
against the left hip alighted with the agile abandon of a
cat on hot bricks. This was Lord Emsworth's brother
Galahad, and he moved briskly at all times because he
always felt so well. He was too elderly to be rejoicing in
his youth, but he gave the impression of rejoicing in
something.

A niece of his had once commented on this.[11]

'It really is an extraordinary thing,' she had said, 'that
anyone who has had such a good time as he has can be
so frightfully healthy. Everywhere you look you see men
leading model lives and pegging out in their prime, but
good old Uncle Gally, who apparently never went to bed
till he was fifty, is still breezing along as fit and rosy as
ever.'

Galahad Threepwood was the only genuinely
distinguished member of the family of which Lord
Emsworth was the head. Lord Emsworth himself had
once won a first prize for pumpkins at the Shropshire
Agricultural Show, and his Berkshire sow, Empress of
Blandings, had three times been awarded the silver
medal for fatness, but you could not say that he had
really risen to eminence in the public life of England.
But Gally had made a name for himself. There were men
in London – bookmakers, skittle sharps, jellied eel
sellers on race courses, and men like that – who would

not have known whom you were referring to if you had mentioned Einstein, but they all knew Gally. He had been, till that institution passed beyond the veil, a man at whom the old Pelican Club pointed with pride, and had known more policemen by their first names than any man in the metropolis.[12]

After paying and tipping Jno Robinson and enquiring after his wife, family and rheumatism, for in addition to being fit and rosy he had a heart which was not only of gold but in the right place, he made his way to the butler's pantry, eager after his absence in London to get in touch with Sebastian Beach, for eighteen years the castle's major domo.[13] He and Beach had been firm friends since, as he put it, they were kids of forty.

Beach welcomed him with respectful fervour and produced port for which after his long train journey he was pining, and for a while all was quiet except for the butler's bullfinch,[14] crooning meditatively to itself in its cage on the window sill. The sort of port you got in Beach's pantry if you were as old a friend as Gally was did not immediately encourage conversation, but had to be sipped in reverent silence. Eventually Gally spoke. Having uttered an enthusiastic 'Woof!' in appreciation of the elixir, he said:

'Well, Beach, let's have all the news. How's Clarence?'

'His lordship is in good health, Mr Galahad.'

'And the Empress?'

'Extremely robust.'

'Clarence still hanging on her lightest word?'

'His lordship's affection has suffered no diminution.'

'Of course it wouldn't have. I keep forgetting that it's only a week since I was here.'[15]

'Was it agreeable in London, sir?'

'Not very. Have you ever noticed, Beach, how your views change as the years go by? There was a time when you had to employ wild horses to drag me from London, and they had to spit on their hands and make a special effort. And now I can't stand the place. Gone to the dogs since they did away with hansom cabs and spats. Do you realize that not a single leg in London has got a spat on it today?'

'Very sad, sir.'

'A tragedy. Except for an occasional binge like the annual dinner of the Loyal Sons of Shropshire, which was what took me up there this time, I have shaken the dust of London from my feet. I shall settle down at Blandings and grow a long white beard. The great thing about Blandings is that it never changes. When you come back to it after a temporary absence, you don't find they've built on a red-brick annexe to the left wing and pulled down a couple of the battlements. A spot more of the true and blushful, Beach.'

'Certainly, Mr Galahad.'

'Of course one sees new faces. Pig men come and go. The boy who cleans the knives and boots is not always the same. Dogs die and maids marry. And, arising from that, who was the girl I passed on my way through the hall? She reminded me of someone I knew in the old days who used to dive off roofs into tanks of water. Daredevil Esmeralda she called herself. She subsequently married a man in the hay, corn and feed business. Who is this girl? Blue eyes and brown hair. She's new to me.'

'That would be her ladyship's maid, Marilyn Poole, Mr Galahad.'

'Ladyship? What ladyship?'

'Lady Diana, sir.'

Galahad, who had started and stiffened at the word 'ladyship', drew a relieved breath. He was very fond of his sister Diana, the only one of his many sisters with whom he was on cordial terms. When he had left the castle, it had been a purely male establishment, Lord Emsworth and himself its only occupants; and though he would have preferred it to remain so, if it was only Diana who had muscled in, he had no complaints to make. It might so easily have been Hermione or Dora or Julia or Florence.

'So Lady Diana's here, is she?' he said.

'Yes, sir. She arrived shortly after Lady Florence.'

Gally's monocle fell from his eye.[16]

'You aren't telling me *Florence* is here?' he quavered.

'Yes, Mr Galahad. Also her stepdaughter, Miss Victoria Underwood.'

Gally was a resilient man. His monocle might have become detached from the parent eye at the news that Blandings Castle housed his sister Florence, but this further piece of information did much to restore his customary euphoria. Florence, widow of the wealthy J. B. Underwood, the American millionaire, might be a depressant, but his niece Vicky's company he always enjoyed.[17]

'How was she?' he asked.

'Her ladyship seemed much as usual.'

'Not Lady Florence. Vicky.'

'Somewhat depressed, I thought.'

'I must cheer her up.'

'Sir James Piper is also a guest.'

This final news item brought a further ray of sunshine to Gally's mood. Only the fear of choking on Beach's superb port prevented him uttering a glad cry.

'Old Jimmy Piper!' he said when he was at liberty to speak. 'I haven't seen him for years. I used to know him well. Sad how time ruins old friendships. What is he now? Prime Minister or something, isn't he?'

'Chancellor of the Exchequer, sir, I understand.'

'He's come on a lot since we were fellow members of the Pelican. I remember young Jimmy Piper used constantly to be chucked out of the old Gardenia.[18] I

suppose he's had to give up all that sort of thing now.
That's the curse of getting to the top in politics. You
lose your *joie de vivre*. I don't suppose Jimmy has been
thrown out of a restaurant for years. But mark you,
Beach, he is more to be pitied than censured. Just as he
was at his best a ghastly sister came to live with him
and changed his whole outlook. That's why we drifted
apart. I looked him up one day, all agog for one of our
customary frolics, and the sister was there and she froze
me stiff. We could have met at his club, of course, in fact
he asked me to lunch there, but when I found that his
club was the Athenæum,[19] crawling, as you probably
know, with bishops and no hope of anyone throwing
bread at anyone, I bowed out. And I've not seen him
since. The right thing to do, don't you think? Making a
clean cut of it. The surgeon's knife. But it will be
delightful seeing Jimmy again. I hope he hasn't brought
his sister with him.'

'He has, Mr Galahad.'

'What!'

'Or, rather, Miss Piper is expected in a few days.'

'Oh, my God! Does Clarence know?'

'His lordship has been informed.'

'How did he take it?'

'He appeared somewhat disturbed.'

'I don't wonder. Blandings Castle seems to be filling
up like the Black Hole of Calcutta, and a single guest
gives him a sinking feeling. Where is he?'

'At the Empress's sty, I presume, Mr Galahad.'

'I must go to him immediately and do my best to
console him. A pretty figure I should cut in the eyes of
posterity if I were to sit here swilling port while my only
brother was up to his collar stud in the slough of
despond.'

And so saying Gally leaped to the door.

He had scarcely reached the outer air when a small
but solid body flung itself into his arms with a squeal of

welcome. Victoria (Vicky) Underwood was always glad to see her Uncle Galahad, and never more so than at a time when, as Beach had said, she was somewhat depressed.

3

Uncles occasionally find their nephews trying and are inclined to compare them to their disadvantage with the young men they knew when they were young men, but it is a very rare uncle who is unable to fraternize with his nieces. And of all his many nieces Gally was fondest of Vicky. She was pretty, a girl whom it was a pleasure to take to race meetings and garden parties, and she had that animation which in his younger days he had found so attractive in music hall artistes and members of the personnel of the chorus.[20]

This animation was missing now. After that tempestuous greeting she had relapsed into a melancholy which would have entitled her to step straight into one of those sombre plays they put on for one performance on Sunday afternoons, and no questions asked. Gally gazed at her, concerned. Beach, that shrewd diagnostician, had been right, he felt, though his 'somewhat depressed' had been an understatement. Here was plainly a niece whose soul had been passed through the wringer, a niece who had drained the bitter cup and, what is more, had found a dead mouse at the bottom of it. Her demeanour reminded him of a girl he had once taken to Henley Regatta – at the moment when she had discovered that a beetle had fallen down the back of her summer sports wear.

'What on earth's the matter?' he asked.

'Nothing.'

'Don't be an ass,' said Gally irritably. 'You're

obviously as down among the wines and spirits as
Mariana at the moated grange.'[21]

'I'm all right, except that I wish I was dead.'

'Were dead, surely,' said Gally, who was a purist.
'What do you want to be dead for? Great Scott!' he
exclaimed, suddenly enlightened. 'Have you been
jugged? Are you doing a stretch? Is that why you're at
Blandings?'

The question did not display such amazing intuition
as anyone unfamiliar with Blandings Castle might have
supposed. All old English families have their traditions,
and the one most rigorously observed in the family to
which Vicky belonged ruled that if a young female
member of it fell in love with the wrong man she was
instantly shipped off to Blandings, there to remain until
she came, as the expression was, to her senses.

Young male members who fell in love with the wrong
girls were sent to South Africa, as Gally had been thirty
years ago. It was all rather unpleasant for the lovelorn
juveniles, but better than if they had been living in the
Middle Ages, when they would probably have had their
heads cut off.

Gally, taking for granted that the reply to his
question would be in the affirmative, became
reminiscent.

'Lord love a duck,' he said emotionally, 'it seems only
yesterday that they had me serving a term in the lowest
dungeon below the castle moat because of Dolly
Henderson.'[22]

Feminine curiosity momentarily overcame Vicky's
depression. She knew vaguely that there had been some
sort of trouble with Uncle Gally centuries ago, and she
was glad to be about to get the facts.

'Were you imprisoned at Blandings?'

'With gyves upon my wrists.'

'I thought you were sent to South Africa.'

'Later, after I had been well gnawed by rats.'

'Who was Dolly Henderson?'

'Music halls. She sang at the old Oxford and the Tivoli.'

'Tights?'

'Pink. And she was the only woman I ever wanted to marry.'

'Poor Gally.'

'Yes, it was rather a nasty knock when my father bunged a spanner into the works. You never knew him, did you?'

'I met him once when I was a very small child. He paralysed me.'

'I don't wonder. That voice, those bushy eyebrows. You must have thought you were seeing some sinister monster out of a fairy story.[23] Clarence is a great improvement as head of the family. If I told Clarence I wanted to marry somebody, there wouldn't be any family curses and thumping of tables; he would just say "Capital, capital, capital", and that would be that. But don't let's talk about me. Are you very much in love?'

'Yes.'

'What's his name?'

'Jeff Bennison.'

'Any money?'

'No.'

'Which of course makes your stepmother shudder at the sight of him.'

'She's never seen him.'

'But she would shudder if she did. Lack of the stuff is always the rock on which the frail craft of love comes a stinker where Blandings Castle is concerned.'

'And there's another thing.'

'What is that?'

'Jeff's an artist.'

Gally looked grave. To his sister Florence, he knew, an artist would be automatically suspect. *La vie de Bohème*, she would say to herself. Uninhibited goings-on at the Bohemian Ball. Nameless orgies in the old studio. Now more than ever he saw how grievously the cards were stacked against this young couple, and his heart went out to them.

'He started as an architect, but his father lost all his money and he couldn't carry on. So he tried to make a living painting, but you know how it is. Poor darling, he has had to take a job teaching drawing at a girls' school.'[24]

'Good God!'

'Yes, I think that's how he feels about it. Do you mind if I leave you now, Gally? I feel a flood of tears coming on.'

'I am open at the moment to be cried in front of.'

'No, I'd rather be alone.'

'I'm sorry. I was hoping I could do something to cheer you up. But naturally at a time like this you don't want an old gargoyle like me hanging around.'

Gally proceeded on his way, brooding. He would have given much to have been able to do something to brighten life for the unfortunate girl, but no inspiration came beyond a vague determination to speak to his sister Florence like a Dutch uncle, and he was given the opportunity of doing this as he crossed the lawn which led to the Empress's residence. Florence was there, reading a book in the hammock under the big cedar tree which he, though there was no actual ruling on the point, had always looked on as his own property. Many of his deepest thoughts had come to him when on its cushions, and it was with a sense of outrage that he drew up beside it. If people went about pinching one's personal hammock, he felt, what were things coming to?

'Comfortable?' he said.

Florence looked up from her book, expressing no pleasure at seeing him.

'Oh, you're back, Galahad? Did you enjoy yourself in London?'

'Never mind about my enjoying myself in London,' said Gally as sternly as any uncle that ever came out of Holland. 'I've just been talking to Vicky.'

'Oh?'

'She's upset.'

'Oh?'

'Crying buckets, poor child.'

'Oh?'

'She tells me you object to this dream man of hers.'

'I do. Very strongly.'

'Although you've never seen him. Just because he's short of money. As if everybody wasn't nowadays except Clarence and you. Your late husband must have left you enough to sink a ship. Didn't he leave Vicky any?'

'He did. I'm the trustee for it.'

'And sitting on it like a buzzard on a rock, I gather. What's wrong with this fellow she wants to marry? Is he a criminal of some kind?'

'Probably. His father was.'

'What do you mean?'

'Didn't she tell you his name?'

'Jeff something.'

'Bennison. His father was Arthur Bennison.'

'So what?'

'Have you never heard of Arthur Bennison? It was the great sensation years ago.'

'I must have been out of England. What did he do? Murder somebody?'

'No, just swindled all the people who had invested in his companies. My first husband was one of them. He left the country to avoid arrest and took refuge in one of those South American republics where they don't have extradition. He died five years ago. So now perhaps you can see why I don't want Victoria to marry his son.'

Gally shook his head.

'I don't get it. Is that all you've got against him?'

'Isn't it enough?'

'Not from where I sit. You might just as well refuse to associate with yourself because you had a father like ours.'

'Father was a bully and a tyrant, but he didn't swindle people.'

'Probably because he didn't think of it. As a matter of fact, you know perfectly well that swindling fathers have nothing to do with your objection to Vicky's young man. What gashes you like a knife is his being short of cash. You're a hard woman, Florence. What you need are a few quarts of the milk of human kindness. Look at the way you're treating that husband of yours. Driving him out into the snow and bringing his clipped moustache in sorrow to the grave. Who do you think you are? *La belle dame sans merci* or something?'

Florence picked up her book.

'Oh, go away, Galahad. You're impossible.'

'Just off. I can't bring you another cushion?'

'No, thanks.'

'I've heard it said that lying in a hammock is bad for the spine.'

'Who did you hear it said by?'

'A doctor at the Pelican Club.'

'I suppose all members of the Pelican Club were half-witted.'

Gally withdrew. He was thinking as he resumed his search for his brother Clarence that talking like a Dutch uncle to somebody was all right unless that somebody happened to be a Dutch aunt.

4

He found Lord Emsworth, as he had expected, drooping over the Empress's sty like a wet sock and gazing at its occupant with a rapt expression.

His devotion to the silver medallist had long been the occasion for adverse comment from his nearest and dearest. His severest critic, his sister Constance, was now in America, but there were others almost equally outspoken.

'Old girl,' his brother-in-law Colonel Wedge had said on one occasion to his wife Hermione, returning late at night from a visit to London, 'we've got to face it, Clarence is dotty. Where do you think I found him just now? Down at the pig sty. I noticed something hanging over the rail and thought the pig man must have left his overalls there, and then it suddenly reared itself up and said "Ah, Egbert". Gave me a nasty shock. Questioned as to what he was doing there at that time of night, he said he was listening to his pig.[25] And what, you will ask, was the pig doing? Singing? Reciting "Dangerous Dan McGrew"? Nothing of the kind. Just breathing.'

Nor had Gally, fond though he was of his brother, abstained from criticism.

'I have been closely associated with Clarence for more than half a century, and I know him from caviar to nuts,' had been his verdict. 'His IQ is about thirty points lower than that of a not too agile-minded jellyfish. Capital chap, though. One of the best.'

As Gally approached, he peered at him with a puzzled look on his face, as if he knew he had seen him before somewhere, but could not think where.

With an effort he identified him and gave him a
brotherly nod.

'Ah, Galahad.'

'Ah to you, Clarence, with knobs on.'

'You're here, eh?'

'Yes, right here.'

'Someone told me you had gone to London.'

'I've come back.'

'Come back. I see. Come back, you mean. Yes, quite.
What did you go to London for?'

'Primarily to attend the Loyal Sons of Shropshire
dinner. But I heard that a pal of mine was in a nursing
home with a broken leg, so I stayed on to cheer him up.'

'Nasty thing, a broken leg.'

'Yes, it annoyed Stiffy a good deal.'

'It was he who broke his leg?'

'Yes. Friend of mine from the old Pelican days. Stiffy
Bates.'

'How did he break his leg?'

'Getting off an omnibus.'

'He should have taken a cab.'

'Yes, he'll know better next time.'

They brooded in silence for a while, their thoughts
busy with the ill-starred Stiffy. Then Gally, though
nothing could be more enjoyable than this exchange of
ideas on the subject of broken legs, felt that it was time
for the condolences which he had come to deliver.
Stiffy Bates might have his leg in plaster, but how much
more in need of cheering up was a man who would
shortly have Jimmy Piper's sister Brenda staying with
him.

'And while I was cheering Stiffy up, I ran into Kevin
and had to cheer him up too. I was busy for days.'

'Who is Kevin?'

'Come, come, Clarence, this is not worthy of your
lightning brain. Kevin Moresby, Florence's husband.'

The words 'Who is Florence?' trembled on Lord

Emsworth's lips, but he was able to choke them back and substitute 'And why did Kevin need cheering up?'

'Because he and Florence are separated. She has cast him off like a used tube of toothpaste, and he doesn't like it. I don't know why,' Gally added, for it was his private opinion that Kevin was in luck.

'I never approved of that marriage,' said Lord Emsworth.

'It was entirely unexpected.'

'Most.'

It was about a year since Florence, left a widow by the death of J. B. Underwood, and inheriting from him several million dollars, had startled a good many people by marrying the very handsome but impoverished Kevin Moresby, referred to in the press as 'the playwright'. Kevin was one of those dramatists who start when very young with a colossal hit and cannot repeat. His last seven plays had been failures, and Florence's money had been a welcome windfall. It was easy to imagine what a blow their separation must have been to him.

'Married her for her money, I've always thought,' said Lord Emsworth.

'The same idea occurred to me,' said Gally.

'This is grave news,' he continued, 'about Jimmy Piper's sister.'

'Who is Jimmy Piper?'

'He's staying here.'

'Ah yes, I think I may have seen him. Has he a sister?'

'Yes, and . . . Haven't you heard?'

'Not to my recollection. What about her?'

On the point of answering the question, Gally paused. His brother, he perceived, had completely forgotten what he had been told about the Brenda menace. It was his custom to forget in a matter of minutes anything said to him. It would not be humane, Gally felt, to spoil his day by refreshing his memory. Let him be happy while he could.

'I can't remember,' he said. 'Somebody told me something about her but it's slipped my mind. The Empress looks as fit as ever,' he added, to change the subject.

'She is in wonderful health.'

'Eating well?'

'Magnificently. It's too bad that I can't get anyone to paint her portrait.[26] I did think it would be plain sailing when Connie went to America, but all the prominent artists I have approached have refused the commission.'[27]

To add a likeness of the Empress to those of his ancestors in the Blandings Castle portrait gallery had long been Lord Emsworth's dream, and with the departure of his sister Constance, the spearhead of the movement in opposition to the scheme, his hopes had risen high. The difficulty was to find a suitable artist. All the leading Royal Academicians to whom he had applied had informed him rather stiffly that they did not paint pigs. They painted sheep in Scottish glens, children playing with kittens and puppies, still-life representations of oranges and bananas on plates, but not pigs.

Gally had always approved of the idea, arguing that the Empress could not but lend tone to a gallery filled with the ugliest collection of thugs he had ever had the misfortune to see, comparable only to the Chamber of Horrors at Madame Tussaud's.[28] He made but one exception, the sixth Earl, who he said reminded him of a charming pea and thimble man with whom he had formed a friendship one afternoon at Hurst Park race course the year Billy Buttons won the Jubilee Cup.

'They were very firm about it,' said Lord Emsworth. 'Some of them were quite rude.'

'Egad!' said Gally.

'Eh?' said Lord Emsworth.

'Just egad, Clarence. I've had an inspiration.'

At the word 'portrait' a close observer would have noticed a sudden sparkle in the eye behind Gally's black-rimmed monocle. This usually happened when he got a bright idea.

'Why waste time on Royal Academicians?' he said. 'A lot of stuffed shirts. You don't need what you call a prominent artist. You want an eager young fellow all vim and ginger, and I've got the very man for you. He specializes in pigs.'

'You don't say, Galahad! What's his name?'

'You wouldn't know his name.'

'Is he good?'

'I believe his morals are excellent.'

'At painting, I mean.'

'Terrific.'

'Is he very expensive?'

'He won't charge you a penny. He is very well off, and only paints pigs because he loves them.'

'Is he free at the moment?'

'That is what I shall ascertain when I run up to London tomorrow.'

'My dear Galahad, you can't run up to London tomorrow. You only came back today.'

'What of that? If a man can't run up to London because he has just run down from it, where can he run up to? I want to do you a good turn.'

'It's extremely kind of you, Galahad.'

'Just my old boy scout training, Clarence. One never quite loses the urge to do one's daily good deed.'

Gally walked back to Vicky.

'I think I'll run up to London and interview this young man of yours, to see if he's worthy of you. What's his name besides Jeff?'

'Bennison. But you'll have to run further than London. His school's at Eastbourne.'

'Odd how these schools all flock to the east coast.[29]

It's like one of those great race movements of the Middle Ages. Were you at Eastbourne?'

'Yes, at Dame Daphne Winkworth's,[30] only she wasn't a Dame then. That's where Jeff is.'

'Oh my God. I hope I don't run into her. She was a guest at Blandings not long ago,[31] and our relations were none too cordial. It would be embarrassing to meet her again. But I'll risk it for your sake.'

'What an angel you are, Gally. I'll give you a letter to take to Jeff. My correspondence is closely watched.'

'So was mine. It's the first move of the prison authorities.'

5

Thanks to the absence of his employer Claude Duff had got the day off and was on his way to the fashionable girls' school outside Eastbourne to pay his respects to his aunt Dame Daphne Winkworth, its proprietress. His journey had been uneventful and would not merit attention but for the fact that he happened to share a compartment with Gally, who soon established cordial relations with him. Gally was always a great talker to strangers on trains.

Claude was tall and as aggressively good-looking as a film-star. His clothes were impeccable, for he was particular about the way he looked. At school, where he had shared a study with Jeff Bennison, he had always been pained by the casualness of the latter's costume. When visiting his aunt, he took especial pains to have everything just right, and he was flicking a speck of dust off his left trouser leg when there came out of the front door a stalwart young man, the sight of whom caused him to stare, to blink, and finally to utter a glad cry of 'Bingo!'

It was an embarrassing moment for Jeff. He recognized his old schoolmate without difficulty, but he had no recollection of what his nickname was. And when an old friend has hailed you as 'Bingo', you cannot be formal. He compromised by calling Claude nothing. So when Claude said he was blowed and that Jeff was the last chap he had expected to see coming out of a girls' school, he merely replied that he worked there.

'You work here? How do you mean?'

'I teach drawing.'

'Somebody told me you were an architect.'

'I had to give it up. No money.'

'Oh, I say! That's too bad.'

'Just one of those things. What are you doing now?'

'I'm second secretary to Sir James Piper.'

'The name seems familiar.'

'Chancellor of the Exchequer.'

'Golly, you're moving in exalted circles. How do you like your job?'

'Very much. How do you like teaching drawing?'

'I don't like it. Or didn't. Recently – in fact this morning – I have been relieved of my duties.'

'Eh?'

'Sacked. Fired. Given the push. I had a dispute with the boss and lost my temper.'

'Gosh! Aunt Daphne wouldn't like that.'

'She didn't. So she's your aunt, is she?'

'Yes.'

'Sooner you than me.'

'What will you do now?'

'Look around, I suppose, till I find something worthy of my talents. But I mustn't stand talking to you. I must go and finish my packing. She wants me off the place at my earliest convenience. Or sooner.'

Left alone, Claude stood musing. He was a goodhearted young man, and Jeff's predicament had saddened him. He himself had never had to worry about money. His father had pushed him into this secretarial job, thinking it would lead to all sorts of things – if he wanted to go into Parliament, for instance – but if Sir James ever decided to part company with him he had several rich relations ready to give him employment. But Jeff, who had been his hero at school . . . he didn't like the look of Jeff's position at all.

He was still brooding and was liking the position less than ever, when the dapper little man he had met on the train came trotting up.[32] Glad of anything which would divert his gloomy thoughts, he greeted him effusively, and the little man seemed equally pleased to see him.

'We meet again,' he said. 'Did I finish that story of mine about my friend Fruity Biffen and the Assyrian beard?[33] I fancy not. It was one he bought at Clarkson's in order to be able to attend the Spring meeting at Newmarket and at the same time avoid recognition from the various bookies he owed money to. And he was just passing the stall of Tim Simms, the Safe Man, when it fell off. Something wrong with the gum, one supposes.'

'Was Simms one of the ones he owed money to?'

'One of the many, and there was a painful scene. But Fruity's life was never what you would call placid. I remember one morning asking him to come for a walk in the park with me. It was at the epoch when I was rather addicted to feeding the ducks on the Serpentine. He was horrified. "Me out of doors on a Monday in the daytime!" he gasped. "You must be mad. If only Duff and Trotter will trust me for a couple of raised pies[34] and a case of old brandy, I intend hiding in the crypt of St Paul's till the bookies have forgotten all about the City and Suburban." Did you tell me, by the way, that your name was Duff?'

'That's right.'

'Any relation to Duff and Trotter, the provision people?'

'My uncle.'

'Then you ought to be all right for raised pies. Galahad Threepwood at this end. Do you come to this seminary often?'

'Fairly often.'

'Then perhaps you can help me. How do I find a fellow called Bennison?'

Claude was all animation.

'Jeff Bennison? Old Bingo? I've just been talking to him. One of my oldest friends.'

'Really?'

'He's gone up to his room.'

'Then I will follow him.'

Jeff, his packing finished, had left his room. Dame Daphne's butler met him at the foot of the stairs.

'There is a gentleman to see you, Mr Bennison,' he said. 'I have shown him to the morning room.'

Gally was polishing his eyeglass when Jeff joined him in the morning room, as always when ill at ease. He was not a man to be readily unnerved, but even he quailed a little now that he was in such close proximity to Dame Daphne Winkworth.

'Mr Bennison?' he said. 'How do you do. My name is Threepwood. You must pardon me for being agitated.'

'You don't seem agitated to me.'

'I wear the mask, do I? I am agitated, though. I am in the position of a native of India who knows that a tigress is lurking in the undergrowth near at hand and wonders how soon she will be among those present. I allude to Dame Daphne Winkworth. No danger of her dropping in, is there?'

'I shouldn't think so.'

'Good. Then we can proceed. I come bringing a letter from my niece Victoria. I am her Uncle Galahad.'

'Oh, how do you do?' said Jeff. 'I've heard her talk of you.'

'No doubt she has a fund of good stories. Here's the letter.'

'You don't mind if I kiss it?'

'I shall be offended if you don't.'

'And if I then skim through it for a moment?'

'Go ahead.'

It was some little time before Jeff was able to resume the conversation.

'Thank God you brought me this,' he said at length. 'I've been worrying myself into a decline. I kept writing to her, but no answer.'

'I doubt if she got your letters.'

'I sent them to her London address.'

'Then they were probably forwarded to Blandings
Castle, where she now is, and intercepted and destroyed.
I'd better sketch out for you the position of affairs
concerning you and Vicky and the Blandings Castle
circle. Finding out about your romance, my sister
Florence instantly had Vicky arrested and hauled off to
the clink. In other words, she was taken to Blandings.
This, I may say, is always done when girls of my family
fall in love with men whom their mothers consider
undesirable. It's a matter of money, of course. Unless the
chap has a solid balance at the bank, he automatically
becomes undesirable. You, I gather from Vicky, have
nothing but your salary here.'

'Not even that. I've just been fired.'

'Really? Too bad.'

'A merciful release I looked on it as. The thought that
I shall never have to see another school-girl trying to
draw is like a tonic. Of course, the situation has its
disadvantages. I expect to starve in the gutter at any
moment.'

'No money?'

'Very little.'

'No prospects?'

'Only hopes. It's like this. If you're Vicky's Uncle
Galahad, you must be my friend Freddie Threepwood's[35]
Uncle Galahad.'

'Remorselessly true, but I don't see where you're
heading.'

'I mean you know all about Freddie, that he's out in
America selling dog-biscuits and has become a regular
tycoon and knows everybody – editors and people like
that.'

'I believe he's doing very well. He took the
precaution of starting his career by marrying the boss's
daughter.'

'He was in England not long ago. They sent him over to buck up the English end of the business.'

Gally, who, like all confirmed *raconteurs*, was not good at listening patiently to other people's stories, heaved a sigh.

'I'm sure this narrative is getting somewhere,' he said, 'but I wish you would tell me where.'

'I'm coming to the nub. The last time he was in England I gave him a comic strip I'd done to try to sell to some paper over there. You know those comic strips – Mutt and Jeff, Blondie, all that. They go on for ever, and it means big money. I'll be on velvet if he sells it.'

'He's bound to. There are no limits to the powers of a man capable of selling dog-biscuits. But meanwhile you will probably be glad of a job to keep you from starving in that gutter you spoke of.'

'I certainly would.'

'Then listen carefully and I'll tell you how this can be arranged.'

Whatever Gally's defects – and someone like his sister Hermione[36] could speak of these by the hour, scarcely pausing to take in breath – he could tell a story well, and long before the conclusion of his résumé of recent events at Blandings Castle, Jeff had gathered that he was to become the latest of the long line of impostors who had sneaked into that stately home of England.

'You have no objection to becoming an impostor?'[37]

'I shall enjoy it.'

'I felt sure you would say so. One can see at a glance that you have the same spirit of adventure that animated Drake, Stanley, and Doctor Livingstone and is the motive power of practically all cats. You'll like Blandings. Gravel soil, company's own water, extensive views over charming old-world parkland. You will, moreover, be constantly in the society of my brother Clarence and his monumental pig, which alone is worth the price of admission. And now think of a name.'

'For me?'

'It would hardly be within the sphere of practical politics to use your own, considering that my sister Florence writhes like an electric eel at the very sound of it. David Lloyd-George? Good, but still not quite what we want. Messmore Breamworthy?'

'Could there be a name like that?'

'It is the name of one of Freddie's co-workers at Donaldson's Dog Joy, Long Island City, USA. But I don't really like it. Too ornate, and the same objection holds in the case of Aubrey Trefusis, Alexander Strong-in-th'-Arm and Augustus Cave-Brown-Cave. We need something simple, easily remembered. Wibberley-Smith? I like the Smith. We'll settle on that. Bless my soul,' said Gally with fervour, 'how it brings back old triumphs, this sketching out plans for adding another impostor to the Blandings roll of honour. But the thing has rather lost its tang since Connie went to America. The man who could introduce an impostor into the castle under Connie's X-ray eye and keep him there undetected had done something he could be proud of. "This," he could say to himself, "was my finest hour!"'

6

The journey from Eastbourne to Market Blandings is a
long and tiring one, but Gally's wiry frame was more
than equal to it, and he alighted at his destination in
good shape. He was, however, afflicted by a thirst which
could not wait to be slaked by Beach's port, and he made
his way to the Emsworth Arms[38] for a beaker of the
celebrated beer brewed by G. Ovens, its proprietor.
Arriving at the bar, he found his old friend James Piper
there, and was saddened to see that he looked as gloomy
as ever.

Sir James had been a disappointment to Gally ever
since the latter's return to Blandings Castle. He had not
expected to find the sprightly young Jimmy Piper of the
old Pelican days, for he knew that long years in
Parliament, always having to associate with the sort of
freaks who get into Parliament nowadays, take their toll;
but he had anticipated a reasonable cheerfulness, and
such was Jimmy's moroseness that it could not be
explained merely by the circumstance of his having
perpetually on the back of his neck a sister like Brenda.
After all, Gally felt, he himself had ten sisters,[39] four of
them just as bad as Brenda, but you never heard
unmanly complaints from him.

Gally was not a man to beat about bushes. He
welcomed this opportunity of solving a mystery which
had been annoying him, and embarked on his probe
without preamble.

'What on earth's the matter with you, Jimmy? And
don't say "Nothing" or talk a lot of guff about the cares
of office weighing on you. A man doesn't necessarily go

about looking like a dead fish because he's Home
Secretary, or whatever you are. I've known Home
Secretaries who were as cheerful as stand-up comics.
No, something is biting you, and I want to know what it
is. Confide in me, Jimmy, bearing in mind that there
was a time when our minds were open books to each
other. You've given me enough material to write your
biography, only I suppose it wouldn't do now that you
are such a big pot. Still, let's have the latest
instalments.'

It was only for a moment that Sir James hesitated.
Then, for G. Ovens's home-brew has above all other
beverages the power to break down reticences, he said:

'Can I confide in you, Gally?'

'Of course.'

'I badly need advice.'

'I have it on tap.'

'You remember in the old days how crazy I was about
your sister Diana?'

'I remember.'

'I still am. You'd think I would have got over it, but
no. The moment I saw her again, it was just as bad as
ever.'

His statement was one which might have seemed
sensational to some auditors, but Gally took it calmly.
He had the advantage of having given up many hours of
his valuable time to listening to a younger James Piper
expressing himself on the subject of the woman he
loved; and if he was surprised, it was only because he
found it remarkable that the fire of those days should
still be ablaze after all those years.

That his sister Diana should be the object of this
passion occasioned him no astonishment. He had always
placed her in the top ten for looks, charm and general
espièglerie and had shared in the universal consternation
when she had thrown herself away on an ass like Rollo
Phipps.

'Good for you, Jimmy,' he said. 'If you are trying to find out if I approve, have no anxiety. When the wedding ceremony takes place, you can count on me to be in the ringside pew lending a fairly musical baritone to The Voice That Breathed o'er Eden or whatever hymn you may have selected. Now that Diana has been so satisfactorily de-Phippsed I could wish her no better husband.'

Sir James had imbibed a full tankard of G. Ovens's home-brew and was half way through his second, and that amount of the elixir is generally calculated to raise the spirits of the saddest into the upper brackets, but the cloud remained on his brow, darker than ever.

'The wedding ceremony isn't going to take place,' he said bitterly.

Gally leaped to the obvious conclusion, and his eye glass, as if in sympathy, leaped to the end of its string.

'Don't tell me you've changed your mind.'

'Of course not.'

'Then why this pessimistic outlook? Did she turn you down?'

'I haven't proposed.'

'Why not?'

'I didn't get the chance.'

'I thought you were going to say you discovered you had some incurable disease and had been given two weeks to live, which would of course have spoiled the honeymoon. The trouble with you politicians,' said Gally, 'is that you wrap up your statements to such an extent with double-talk that the lay mind needs an electric drill to get at the meaning.[40] Tell me in a few simple words what the hell you're talking about.'

'I can tell you in one. Murchison.'

'Who's Murchison?'

'My bodyguard.'

'Have you a bodyguard?'

'Sergeant E. B. Murchison. A Chancellor of the

Exchequer has to have a bodyguard, assigned to him by
Scotland Yard.'

Gally shook his head.

'You ought never to have let them make you
Chancellor of the Exchequer, Jimmy. If I had known, I
would have warned you against it. What does this fellow
Murchison do? Follow you around?'

'Wherever I go.'

'You must feel like Mary with her lamb, though I
doubt if anyone attached to Scotland Yard has fleece as
white as snow. I begin to see now. Your style is
necessarily cramped. If you pressed your suit and Diana
proved cooperative, your immediate impulse would be
to fold her in a close embrace, and you wouldn't want a
goggling detective looking on.'

'Exactly. I'm a shy man.'

'Are you?'

'Very shy.'

'That makes it worse. I've never been shy myself, but
I can understand how you feel. No chance of you
stiffening the sinews, summoning up the blood and
having a pop at it regardless of Murchison?'

'None.'

'Then we must think of something else.'

'I have thought of something else. I'm going to write
her a letter.'

'Outlining your sentiments?'

'Yes.'

Gally was not encouraging.

'Dismiss the idea. A letter is never any good,
especially if it's from someone like you, most of whose
adult life has been spent in politics. You've got so
accustomed to exercising caution and not committing
yourself that you simply aren't capable of the sort of
communication which hits a woman like a sock in the
solar plexus and makes her say to herself, "Lord love a
duck, this boy's got what it takes. I must weigh this

proposal of his carefully or I'll be passing up the snip of a lifetime".'

James Piper finished his home-brew and heaved a sigh.

'You make it all seem very hopeless, Gally.'

'Nothing is hopeless, if you have a Galahad Threepwood working for you,' said Gally. 'I have solved problems worse than yours in my time, so buck up and let us see that merry smile of yours that goes with such a bang in the House of Commons.'

7

There were times, it seemed to Gally some days after his heart to heart talk with James Piper at the Emsworth Arms, when the grounds and messuages of Blandings Castle came as near to resembling an enchanted fairyland as dammit. Strong hands had mowed the lawn till it gleamed in the sunlight, birds sang in the tree tops, bees buzzed in the flower beds. You would not be far wrong, he thought, if you said that all Nature smiled, as he himself was doing. His mood was mellow, its mellowness increased by the fact that, slipping adroitly from the table at the conclusion of lunch, he had secured the hammock under the cedar before the slower Florence could get at it. She came out of the house just after he had moved in, and it set the seal on his euphoria to note her thwarted look, comparable to that of baffled baronets in melodramas he had seen at the Lyceum and other theatres in his younger days. It was the keystone of his policy always, if possible, to show his sisters, with the exception, of course, of Diana, that they weren't everybody.

His strategy was effective. Florence took her book elsewhere. But he knew it was too much to expect that his siesta would remain undisturbed indefinitely. Nor did it. Scarcely had his eyes closed and his breathing become deeper, when a respectful finger poked him in the ribs and he woke to see Beach at his side.

'Mr Galahad,' said Beach.

'Ah, Beach, Beach,' he replied, 'I was having a lovely dream about backing a long shot for the Grand National and seeing it come in by a length and a half. Are you here just to have a chat?'

'No, sir,' said Beach, shocked. He would chat freely with Mr Galahad in the seclusion of his pantry, but not on the front lawn. 'A Mr Smith has called, asking to see you.'

For an instant the name conveyed nothing to Gally. Then memory stirred, and he sat up with enthusiasm.

'Bring him along, Beach,' he said. 'Nobody you know, but he's just the fellow I hoped would be calling,' and he was on his feet and prepared to welcome Jeff when Beach produced him, which he did some moments later with what amounted to a flourish. Any friend of Mr Galahad got the VIP treatment from Beach. He then melted away as softly and gracefully as was within the power of a butler who would never see fourteen stone again, and Gally and Jeff were, as the former would have put it, alone and unobserved.

'My dear boy,' said Gally, 'this is splendid. I was half afraid you would lose your nerve and not come.'

'Nothing would have kept me away.'

'You Smiths do not know what fear is?'

'Only by hearsay. Nice place you have here.'

'We like it. But there is a catch. I don't know if you are familiar with the hymn about spicy breezes blowing o'er Ceylon's isle?'

'Where every prospect pleases and only man is vile.'

'Exactly. However, it's the women you have to watch out for, rather than the men. If you had a classical education, you will remember the Gorgon who used to turn people to blocks of ice[41] with a glance. My sister Florence, whom you will be meeting in a moment, is like that when offended.'

'I can see the solution there. I won't offend her.'

'You have already done so. You have come to paint the Empress's portrait, to be added to those in the family portrait gallery, and she is as sick as mud about it. When she is as sick as mud about anything she stiffens from the soles of her feet upwards and gives the offending party the sort of look the Gorgon used to give people. Being her brother and exposed to it from childhood, I am immune to this, but I always warn strangers to be sure to make their wills before getting together with her, just in case. Some people will tell you that she isn't as bad as my sister Connie. How right Kipling was when he made that crack about the female of the species being more deadly than the male. Look at our family. My brother Clarence is as gentle a soul as ever said "What ho!" to a pig, and I, as you must have noticed already, am absolutely charming, but the only one of my sisters whom I would not be afraid to meet down a dark alley is Diana.'

It would be idle to deny that these grave words gave young Mr Smith a disagreeable sinking sensation in the neighbourhood of the third waistcoat button, but love conquers all, as someone once said, and he thought of Vicky and was strong again. He might be about to be turned into a block of ice, but the weather was warm and he would eventually thaw out again and see Vicky once more. He told Gally that his plans were unaltered, and Gally said it did him credit.

'The great thing to bear in mind,' said Gally, 'is that sisters are sent into the world to try us and make us more spiritual. I attribute my own spirituality entirely to having been brought up in the same nursery as Connie and Hermione and Dora. It taught me fortitude and a sense of proportion. When I went out into the great world, I met a variety of tough eggs, but always I was able to say to myself "Courage, Galahad, this egg is unquestionably hard to cope with, but he isn't Connie or Hermione or Dora!" You wouldn't believe the things that went on in that nursery. My sister Hermione once laid me out cold with one blow of her doll Belinda. Am I scaring you?'

'Yes,' said Jeff.

'You quail at the thought of meeting Florence?'

'Yes,' said Jeff.

'But you are prepared to go through it?'

'Yes,' said Jeff.

'Good. Let us hope that this will be one of her good mornings,' said Gally, and he took him to Beach and told Beach to take him to Lady Florence, which Beach did, and Gally returned to his hammock.[42]

Before he could reach it he met Sir James Piper coming across the lawn and was pained to see his careworn aspect. Sir James was looking as an investor in some[43] company might have looked on learning that its managing director had left England without stopping to pack.

'Stap my vitals, Jimmy,' said Gally, 'you look like the Mona Lisa.[44] You remind me of the last time I saw you chucked out of the old Gardenia. The same wan expression as the hand of the Law closed on coat collar and trouser seat. What's wrong? Or needn't I ask?'

'You needn't.'

'The same little trouble you were having when we chatted at the Emsworth Arms?'

'Yes.'

'I'll give you a pep talk.'

'I haven't time for any pep talks. I'm playing croquet[45] with Diana. She's waiting for me now.'

It is always pleasant for a man of good will to be given the chance of bringing the roses back to the cheeks of a stricken friend, and Gally lost no time in availing himself of this one.

'Croquet!' he cried. 'Then, my dear fellow, what on earth are you making heavy weather about? Don't you know that there is no surer way to a woman's heart than that footling game? At least there usedn't to be when I was ass enough to swing a mallet in my youth. In those days eighty per cent of betrothals took place on the

45

croquet lawn. The opportunities for whispering words of love into shell-like ears are endless. If I hadn't been sent to South Africa, where they didn't play, I should have been engaged half a dozen times before I was twenty-five. So buck up, Jimmy. Go ahead and fear nothing. I see you bringing off a sensational triumph.'

'With Murchison looking on?'

Gally's enthusiasm waned perceptibly.

'I'd forgotten Murchison,' he said.

'I hadn't,' said Sir James. 'I never do.'

It was shortly after he had passed on to keep his tryst, with E. B. Murchison following in his footsteps like King Wenceslaus's page, that Gally, back in the hammock and thinking happily how comfortable Florence would have been if she had got there first, was roused from his musings by the arrival of Vicky.

Vicky was looking bewildered, as if strange things had been happening around her which she felt that only Gally with his greater wisdom could explain. Though she was not hopeful that even Gally would be able to find an explanation for what was weighing on her mind at the moment except the unwelcome one that that mind was tottering.

'Gally,' she said, 'do you think you can see things that aren't there?'

'Do you mean ghosts? Clarence's pig man claims to have seen the White Lady of Blandings[46] one Saturday night as he was coming out of the Emsworth Arms at closing time. One cannot, however, dismiss the theory that he was pie-eyed at the time. Why do you ask?'

'Because I've just seen Jeff.'

'Ah, yes.'

'Is that all you can say?'

'You were bound to see him some time, now that he's here.'

'He's *here*?'

'Yes, I got him the job of painting the Empress.'

Vicky uttered what in a girl less attractive would have been a squeal. She was conscious of a weakness about the knees. Her grandmother in similar circumstances would have swooned.

'Gally,' she said, 'I think I'm going to collapse on you.'

'Come along. Plenty of room.'

'Or shall I just gaze at you with adoring eyes?'

'Whichever you prefer. When you meet him, by the way, you must remember to address him as Mister Smith. He is here strictly incognito.'

'I'll remember.'

'Well, mind you do.'

'Don't be afraid I'll let the side down. I've read lots of secret service stories and I know the procedure. I will now,' said Vicky, 'gaze at you with adoring eyes.'

She was proceeding to do so, when a figure, well-knit though inclining to stoutness, appeared on the lawn. Sir James Piper, closely followed by Sergeant E. B. Murchison.

'Hullo,' said Gally as his old friend reached the hammock. 'Finished your croquet already?'

Sir James hastened to dispel any idea he may have had that that leisured pastime had been affected by the modern craze for speed.

'We haven't begun yet.'

'What's the trouble?'

'Diana wanted her large hat.'

'I don't wonder. The sun is very sultry and we must avoid its ultry-violet rays, as the song says.[47] Well, I won't keep you. Don't forget what I told you.'

'What did you tell him?' Vicky asked as Sir James resumed his quest for large hats.

'To push croquet to its logical conclusion.'

'Whatever that means.'

'I will explain when it's cooler.'

'Explain now.'

'It's quite simple. He's in love with your Aunt Diana,

and I was pointing out to him . . . Ah, here he is, complete with hat. You've got that Mona Lisa look again, Jimmy. What's wrong?'

'Nothing's exactly wrong, but I wish Brenda would mind her own business. She's sent my secretary down here in case, she says, I need him.'

'Well, don't you? I would have thought he was the very chap you would want to have around if any weighty thoughts occurred to you. You'd look pretty silly if an idea for balancing the budget occurred to you and you forgot it because there was nobody to take it down in his note book.'

'I'm supposed to be on holiday.'

'You mustn't think so much of holidays, Jimmy. Life is stern and earnest. You ought to be floating loans or whatever it is you do in your job, and a secretary is essential. However, as you seem determined to live for pleasure alone, I will leave you to your croquet.'

'The last thing I want is Claude Duff following me about with his note book. It's bad enough having Murchison. But two of them!'

Words failed Sir James and he passed on, and Gally was so moved that he sat up in the hammock and dropped his eyeglass.

'Claude Duff!' he exclaimed. 'Oh my fur and whiskers!'

'What's the matter?'

'Ruin stares us in the eyeball.'

'Because Claude Duff is here?'

'Exactly.'

'Why?'

'Because,' said Gally, 'he is an intimate friend of your Jeff and will undoubtedly call him by his real name in front of Florence the moment they meet.'

8

The sun was shining as brightly as ever, the birds and bees respectively singing and buzzing with undiminished vigour, but Vicky did not notice them. Her whole attention was monopolized by her Uncle Galahad, who had turned misty and was flickering like an old-time silent picture.

'Oh, Gally,' she wailed. 'Oh, Gally!'

He had no comfort to offer. It was with a sombre look on his face that he retrieved the eyeglass which was dancing on the end of its string.

'You may well say "Oh, Gally",' he said. 'I wouldn't blame you if you made it something stronger.'

'This is frightful!'

'The situation has certainly started to deteriorate.'

'He'll be thrown out.'

'On his ear. "Chuck this man as far as he'll go, and I want to see him bounce twice", Florence will say to the hired help. Unless I have an inspiration.'

'Oh, do try.'

'I am trying, and I think I'm getting the glimmering of an idea. But I shall need a few minutes' solitude if I am to develop it. I can't possibly plot and plan with you having conniption fits at my elbow. Leave me, child, I would be alone. Trot off and pick flowers.'

'How long?'

'Short stalks.'

'I mean how long do you want to be alone?'

'Call it a quarter of an hour.'

'Will that be enough?'

'It should be.'

49

'You're wonderful, Gally.'

'I always was from my earliest years. It's a gift.'

Vicky was one of those girls who are anxious to help. She gave Gally twenty minutes instead of the quarter of an hour he had specified. When she returned to the hammock, she found him so obviously pleased with himself that it was unnecessary to ask questions. She thrilled with relief and for the first time was able to appreciate the efforts of the sun, the birds and the bees, which all this while had been giving of their best.

'I've got it,' said Gally. 'The solution turned out to be a very simple one. I shall see Claude before he meets Jeff and I shall tell him the tale.'

'You'll do what?'

'Tell him the tale.'

'I don't follow you, Mr Threepwood.'

'You don't know what is meant by telling the tale?'

'No.'

'Then in order to explain I shall have to take you back to my impecunious youth, when I combined a taste for wagering on horses with an inability to spot which of the contestants was going to finish first. In a word I was one of the mugs and in constant debt to turf accountants who liked one to settle one's obligations with the minimum of delay. Fortunately I was born with the gift of persuasive eloquence. Mug though I was, I could tell a tale. When at my best, I could make bookies cry and sometimes lend me a fiver to be going along with.'

'What used you to say to them?'

'It wasn't so much what I said as the tone of voice. I had the same knack Sarah Bernhardt had of tearing the heart strings.'

'I hope you were ashamed of yourself.'

'Oh, bitterly.'

'You must have been a very disreputable young man.'

'So I was often told by my nearest and dearest. I was one of those men my mother always warned me against.'

'Well, it's lucky you're such a low character. A saintly uncle wouldn't have been much use in the present crisis. I suppose, when you tell the tale, you deviate from the truth a lot?'

'Quite a good deal. I have always found the truth an excellent thing to deviate from.'

'What are you going to say to Mr Duff?'

'Hullo, Duff. Nice to see you again. Lovely weather, is it not. I shall then give him the works.'

'I can hardly wait.'

'You won't have to, for here he comes, no doubt to report to Jimmy on the croquet lawn.'

This was indeed Claude's purpose, for in addition to being nervous he was conscientious and never shirked his duty, even when unpleasant. His employer, sometimes inclined to be irritable, always gave him the same uneasy feeling as affected him when meeting strange dogs, but he faced him bravely and hoped for the best.

It was, however, without enjoyment that he was going to meet him now, and the sight of Gally, who at their previous encounter had proved so genial a companion, cheered him greatly. So when Gally said 'Hullo, Duff. Nice to see you again. Lovely weather, is it not?' his response was the cordial response of one confident of having found a friend.

'This is Miss Underwood, my niece,' said Gally.

'How do you do?' said Claude.

'How do you do?' said Vicky.

There was a pause. Claude tried to think of a bright remark, but was unable to find one. He regretted this, for Vicky had made a profound impression on him. He substituted a not very bright question.

'Did you find Jeff all right?'

'I did indeed.'

51

'Good old Jeff. I wish I saw more of him.'

'You will. And I should like a word with you before you meet him.'

'Meet him?'

'He's here.'

'What, at the castle?'

'That very spot.'

'That's certainly a surprise. Is he here for long?'

'He won't be if the powers of darkness hear you calling him Jeff.[48] His true identity must be wrapped in a veil of secrecy. Smith is the name to which he answers.'

'I don't understand.'

'I am about to brief you. This incognito stuff is to avoid him being given the bum's rush by my brother Clarence.'

'I still don't . . .'

'You will in a minute. Are you familiar with the facts about Jeff's father?'

'No. What about his father?'

'I shall be coming to that in a moment, but first let me get quite clear as to the relations between you and Jeff. Did I gather correctly from what you were saying when we met at Eastbourne that you and he had been at school together?'

'That's right. Wrykyn.'[49]

'A most respectable establishment.'

'We were in the same house. Our last two years we shared a study.'

'So you were constantly in happy comradeship, now brewing tea and toasting sausages, anon out on the football field, rallying the forwards in the big game.'

'I wasn't in the football team. Jeff was.'

'Or sitting side by side in the school chapel, listening to the chaplain's short manly sermon. What I'm driving at is that, linked by a thousand memories of the dear old school, you wouldn't dream of saying or doing anything to give Jeff a jab in the eye with a burned stick, thus causing him alarm and despondency and rendering his hopes and dreams null and void.'

Claude could not quite follow all the ramifications of this, but he grasped the general import and replied that he could be relied on not to do anything damaging to Jeff's hopes and dreams.

'Good,' said Gally, 'then we can proceed. He is after the job of secretary[50] to my brother Clarence, and his position is a bit tricky. I don't know if you had any difficulty in getting taken on in a similar capacity by Jimmy Piper?'

'No, there wasn't any trouble. My father worked it. He's pretty influential, and he's a great friend of Sir James.'

'How different from Jeff's father. He's dead now, but in his lifetime he was a dishonest financier who ruined hundreds before skipping the country. He did my brother Clarence down for several thousands of the best and brightest, and Clarence is very bitter about it. Clarence, I must tell you, is a man of ungovernable passions, and did he discover that Jeff was the son of the man who got into his ribs for that substantial sum, there would be no question of engaging him as his secretary. He would probably bite him in the leg or throw an ormolu clock or something at him. His fury would be indescribable. That is why I beg you to remember on no account to call Jeff Jeff in his presence. Smith is the name. You understand?'

'Oh, rather.'

'Splendid. What a treat it is dealing with a man of your lightning intelligence. You don't know what a relief it is to feel that we can rely on you. Remember. Not Jeff. Smith. Though as you are such old friends you might call him Smithy.'

'At school we always called him Bingo.'

'That will be capital. Well, I am glad it's all straightened out, my dear Duff. You had now better be getting along and reporting to Jimmy. No doubt he will be delighted to see you.'

Vicky had been listening to these exchanges with growing admiration. As Claude receded in the direction of the croquet lawn, she said:

'At-a-boy, Gally.'

'Thank you, my dear.'

'I see now what you mean by telling the tale.'

'I was not at my best, I fear. One gets a bit rusty as the years go by. Still, it got over all right.'

'Triumphantly.'

'We shan't have any more trouble with Claude Duff. So now there's nothing on our minds.'

'Nothing.'

'We are carefree. We sing tra la la.'

'Would you go as far as that?'

'Omitting perhaps the final la!'

'Though I shall be too nervous to do much singing.'

'Nonsense. Nothing to be nervous about.'

'You really feel that?'

'Certainly. I don't say that when Jimmy told us Claude Duff had clocked in I didn't feel a momentary twinge of uneasiness. But you saw how soon it passed off. What can possibly bung a spanner into our hopes and dreams now? It isn't as if your stepmother was your Aunt Constance. Connie could detect rannygazoo by a sort of sixth sense and smell a rat when all other noses were baffled, but she was a woman in a thousand. Sherlock Holmes could have taken her correspondence course.'

'What a comfort you are, Gally.'

'So I have been told, though not by any of the female members of my family. What a lot of exercise Beach is taking this afternoon,' said Gally, changing the subject as the butler came out of the house and made his way towards them. 'Hullo, Beach. Did you want to see me, or are you out for a country ramble?'

Neither of these suggestions, it appeared, fitted the facts. It was duty that had called Beach to brave the ultra-violet rays of the sun.

'I am taking his lordship a telegram that has just come over the telephone. It is from Mr Frederick, saying that he is in England again and will be paying a visit to the castle as soon as his business interests permit.'

Beach passed on, and Vicky, starting to express her pleasure at the prospect of seeing her Cousin Frederick again, found herself interrupted by a sharp barking sound from her Uncle Galahad, who, becoming coherent, added the words 'Hell's bells!'

'What's the matter?' she asked.

Gally was in no mood to break things gently.

'Do you realize,' he said, his voice choked and his eyeglass once more adrift, 'that we are plunged more deeply in the soup than ever? Freddie is a friend of Jeff's and you know what a bubblehead Freddie is. The chances that he won't call Jeff Jeff in front of your stepmother are virtually nil.'

'Oh, Gally.'

'There is only one thing to do – go to London and intercept him and make him see that he must not come down here. I'll pinch the Bentley[51] and start right away.'

9

Jeff meanwhile, conducted by Beach, had come to journey's end, but he was under no illusion that his pilgrimage was to terminate in lovers' meeting. His emotions on finding himself closeted with Florence somewhat resembled those of a young lion tamer who, entering the lion's cage, suddenly realizes that he has forgotten all he was taught by his correspondence school. A chill seemed to have fallen on the summer day, and he saw how right Gally had been in comparing his sister to the late Gorgon.

Forbidding was the adjective a stylist like Gustave Flaubert would have applied to her aspect, putting it of course in French, as was his habit. She was an angular woman, and her bearing was so erect that one wondered why she did not fall over backwards. She had not actually swallowed some rigid object such as a poker, but she gave the impression of having done so, and Jeff was conscious of surprise that she should have succeeded in getting married to one so notoriously popular with the other sex as J. B. Underwood.[52] Perhaps, he felt, he had proposed to her because somebody betted he wouldn't.

Beach, having announced 'Mr Smith' in a voice from which he did his best to keep the gentle pity he could not but feel for the nice young man he was leaving to face her ladyship in what was plainly one of her moods, withdrew, and Florence opened the conversation.

Some women who at first sight intimidate the beholder set him at his ease with charm of manner. Florence was not one of these. Her 'How do you do', delivered from between clenched teeth, was in keeping with her appearance, and Jeff's morale, already in the low brackets, slipped still lower. No trace remained of the airy confidence with which he had assured Gally that the Smiths knew what fear was only by hearsay. A worm confronted by a Plymouth Rock would have been more nonchalant.

Florence came to the point without preamble.

'I understand that you have come to paint a portrait of Lord Emsworth's pig,' she said, speaking as if the words soiled her lips.

'Yes,' said Jeff, only just checking himself from adding 'ma'am'. It was difficult not to believe himself in the presence of Royalty.

'It is a perfectly preposterous idea.'

There seemed nothing to say in reply to this, so Jeff said nothing. Nobody knew better than himself that he was getting the loser's end of these exchanges, but there seemed nothing he could do about it. He envied Gally, who, he knew, would have taken this haughty woman in his stride.

'Pigs!' said Florence, making it clear that these animals did not stand high in her estimation, and while Jeff was continuing to say nothing the door opened and Lord Emsworth pottered in with his customary air of being a somnambulist looking for a dropped collar stud.

'Florence,' he bleated, 'I've just had a telegram from Frederick. He says he's in England again and is coming here.'

There was no pleasure in his voice. Visits from his younger son seldom pleased him. Freddie was a vice-president of Donaldson's Dog Joy of Long Island City, NY and like all vice-presidents was inclined to talk shop. It is trying for a father who wants to talk about nothing but pigs to have a son in the home who wants to talk about nothing but dog-biscuits.

'Oh?' said Florence.

'I thought you would like to know.'

'I haven't the slightest interest in Frederick's movements.'

'Then you ought to have.'

'Why?'

'You're his aunt.'

If Florence had been less carefully brought up, she would no doubt have said 'So what?' As it was, she chose her words more carefully.

'I am not aware that there is a law, human or divine, which says that an aunt must enjoy the society of a nephew who confines his conversation exclusively to the subject of dog-biscuits.'

'*Noblesse oblige*,' said Lord Emsworth, remembering a good one, and Florence asked him what on earth *noblesse* had got to do with it. As Lord Emsworth was unable to find a reply to this, there was a momentary silence, during which Jeff decided that if there was going to be an argument about what was and what was not required behaviour for aunts, it was a good time to leave. He sidled out, and Lord Emsworth, seeing him for the first time, gazed after him in bewilderment, almost as if, like his pig man, he had been suddenly confronted by the White Lady of Blandings, who was supposed to make her rounds of the castle with her head under her arm, it having been chopped off by her husband in the Middle Ages.

'Who was that?' he asked, and Florence was obliged to soil her lips again.

'Mr Smith,' she said.

'Oh, yes. He's come to paint the Empress.'

'So I understand.'

'He's a friend of Galahad's.'

'I do not consider that a great recommendation.'

'Nice young fellow I thought he looked.'

'He struck me as a criminal type. He's probably known to the police.'

'I don't think so. Galahad said nothing about him being friends of theirs. Odd his disappearing like that. I must find him and take him to see the Empress.'

'Are you really serious about putting that pig's portrait in the portrait gallery?'

'Of course I am.'

'You will be the laughing-stock of the county.'

Gally would have replied that a good laugh never hurt anybody, but Lord Emsworth was more tactful.

'I don't know why you say that. There will be a plaque, don't you call them, at the side of the picture about her being three years in succession silver medallist in the Fat Pigs class at the Shropshire Agricultural Show,[53] an unheard-of feat. People will be too impressed to laugh.'

'A pig among your ancestors!'

'Galahad says she will lend the gallery a tone. He says that at present it is like the Chamber of Horrors at Madame Tussaud's.'

'Don't talk to me about Galahad. The mere mention of his name upsets me.'

'I thought you were having one of your spells. You get them because you're so energetic all the time. You ought to lie in the hammock in the afternoons with a book. Well, I can't stay talking to you all day, I must be going and finding Smith,' said Lord Emsworth.

Jeff was in the corridor, warming up after his session with the Snow Queen. Lord Emsworth greeted him briskly. Already, brief though their acquaintance was, he had taken a great fancy to Jeff.

'Ah, there you are, Mr Smith. I am sorry my sister was having one of her spells when you arrived. She always has them when she starts thinking about putting the Empress's portrait in the portrait gallery. It does something to her. It was the same with my sister Constance, now in America married to an American whose name I have forgotten. She, too, always had these spells when the matter of the Empress's portrait came up. But you will be wanting to see her. Not Constance, the Empress. It is quite a short distance to her sty.'

He led Jeff through the kitchen garden and into a meadow dappled with buttercups and daisies, making pleasant conversation the while.

'Things,' he said, 'have settled down now that the Empress has retired and no longer competes in the Shropshire Agricultural Show, but when she was an active contestant one was never free from anxiety. There was a man living in a house near here who kept entering his pigs for the Fat Pigs event and was wholly without scruples. One always feared that he would kidnap the Empress or do her some mischief which would snatch victory from her grasp. He was a Baronet. Sir Gregory Parsloe.'

Here he paused impressively, seeming to suggest that Jeff must know what baronets were like, and Jeff agreed that they wanted watching, and they reached the sty in perfect harmony.

The Empress was having an in-between-meals snack, her invariable practice when not sleeping, and Jeff regarded her with awe.

'I've never seen such a pig,' he said.

'Nobody has ever seen such a pig,' said Lord Emsworth.

'Good appetite.'

'Excellent. You can't imagine the bran mash she consumes daily.'

'Well, nothing like keeping body and soul together.'

'You would think that anyone would be proud to paint her. And yet all these Royal Academicians refused.'

'Incredible.'

'In fact, my dear fellow, you are my last hope. If you fail me. I shall have to give up the whole thing.'

'I won't fail you,' said Jeff.

He spoke sincerely. The affection Lord Emsworth felt for him was mutual. Say what you might of the ninth Earl – his limpness, the way his trousers bagged at the knees and the superfluity of holes in his shooting jacket – he was essentially a lovable character and Jeff was resolved to do all that was within his power to make him happy. And if the Gorgon objected and had spells, let her have spells.

10

Gally had no difficulty in finding Freddie. A man in London on an expense account generally tends to do himself well, and Freddie, when sent across the Atlantic by his father-in-law to promote the interests of the English branch of Donaldson's Dog Joy, never watched the pennies. It was in a suite at the Ritz that the meeting between uncle and nephew took place. Freddie was having a late breakfast.

Gally was surprised to see a cloud on his nephew's brow, for normally Freddie was a cheerful young man, inclined perhaps, as his Aunt Florence had said, to confine his talk to the subject of dog-biscuits, but uniformly cheerful. His sunny smile, Gally had always understood, was one of the sights of Long Island City, but now it no longer split his face. It was with a moody fork that he pronged the kippered herring on his plate, and not even James Piper could have more closely resembled the Mona Lisa as he sipped coffee.

Gally noted these symptoms with interest. His experienced eye told him that they were not due to a hangover, so it would seem that some business worry was causing this depression.

'Something on your mind, I see,' he said. 'Is it that trade is not brisk?'

'Trade is a pain in the neck,' said Freddie, abandoning the kipper and going on to marmalade. 'In England I mean, not in America. I have not a word of criticism of the American dog, whose appetite for biscuits remains the same as always. But the dogs over here . . . Old Donaldson will have a fit when I turn in my report.'

Gally's face took on a grave expression in keeping with the solemnity of the moment, but he had come here on a mission of vital importance and was not to be diverted from the main issue.

'I'm sorry,' he said, 'but before going into that in depth I will explain why I wanted to see you. Your cousin Victoria –'

'I don't know what England's coming to.'

'Your cousin[54] Victoria has fallen in love with the wrong man and is immured at Blandings, and I have got the man there under a false name. I can reveal this to you without reserve as you have been associated with me in many of my cases. You will recall the Bill Lister incident.'[55]

'And I'll tell you why trade isn't brisk,' said Freddie. 'It's because of the bad practice of English dog owners of giving their dogs scraps at the luncheon and dinner tables. I was lunching –'

'Freddie –'

'I was lunching at a house in Sussex only yesterday, and there was my hostess with a dog on each side of her, and all through the meal she kept giving them hand-outs, yes, even of the Bavarian Cream which was the final course.'

'Freddie –'

'Is it reasonable to suppose that a dog full of Bavarian Cream will be satisfied with a biscuit, even one as wholesome and rich in all the essential vitamins as Donaldson's Dog Joy? Naturally when I produced a sample and offered it to the animals they backed away, turning up their noses, and I was unable to book an order. And the same thing has happened over and over –'

'Freddie,' said Gally, 'if you don't stop babbling about your damned dog-biscuits and listen to me, I'll shove the remains of that kipper down your neck.'

Freddie looked up from his marmalade, surprised.

'Were you saying something?'

63

'I was trying to. It's about Jeff Bennison.'

'I know Jeff Bennison.'

'I know you do.'

'What about him?'

'He and Vicky are in love.'

'Nothing wrong with that, is there?'

'Yes, there is, because Florence has imprisoned her at Blandings to get her out of Jeff's way and I have got Jeff into the house, calling himself Smith.'

'You mean he's in?'

'Yes, he's in.'

'Hob-nobbing daily with Vicky?'

'Yes.'

'Absolutely on the premises?'

'Yes.'

'Then what's your problem?'

'I wouldn't have one if you hadn't wired Clarence that you were coming to Blandings . . . You mustn't come within a hundred miles of the place. Go anywhere else in England that takes your fancy – they say Skegness is very bracing – but keep away from Shropshire.'

'I don't get it. Why?'

'Because the first thing you would do when you got there would be to say – in Florence's presence – "Bless my soul if it isn't my old friend Jeff Bennison. How are you, Jeff old man, how *are* you?"'

Freddie was offended. Had he not been seated, he would undoubtedly have drawn himself up to his full height.

'Are you insinuating that I am a beans-spiller?'

'Yes, I am.'

'I've been given medals for keeping things under my hat.'

'You didn't get one in the Bill Lister affair. I got Bill into the castle incognito in order to oblige my niece Prudence, they being deeply enamoured and kept apart by various relatives. You probably remember the affair . . .'

'Of course I do, and let me tell you –'

'So what occurred? We were all having tea as cosy as be blowed, when you burst in through the french window and bellowed "Blister! Well, well, well! Well, well, well, well, well! This is fine, this is splendid! I can't tell you how glad I am, Prue, that everything is hunky-dory". Then, addressing Prue's mother,[56] you said that Prue could find no worthier mate than good old Bill Lister, whereupon, as might have been foreseen, she had him out of the house in three seconds flat. We don't want that sort of thing happening again.'

If Freddie had not finished his marmalade, he would have choked on it, so great was his indignation.

'Well, dash it,' he thundered, 'I don't see how you can blame me. It stands to reason that if a chap has been established as a pariah and an outcast and you suddenly find him tucking into tea and buttered toast in company with the girl's mother, you naturally assume that the red light has turned to green.'

'Yes, I can see your side of it,' said Gally pacifically. It was no part of his policy to rouse the fiend that slept in Freddie's bosom. 'But I still think it would be safer if you didn't come to Blandings.'

Freddie was all cold dignity.

'I have no wish to come to Blandings,' he said. 'I was only going there to give the guv'nor a treat. He enjoys my visits so much.'

'Then that's settled,' said Gally, relieved. 'A pity, of course, that you won't see Jeff.'

'As a matter of fact,' said Freddie, 'I'm not particularly anxious to see Jeff. He gave me a comic strip thing to sell in America, and I couldn't land it anywhere, and I'm afraid he'll be thinking I've let him down.'

11

By inciting the Bentley to make a special effort Gally was enabled to reach Blandings Castle just in time to dress for dinner. It was not till he joined the company at the table that he became aware that unfortunate things must have been happening in his absence. If the atmosphere was not funereal, he told himself, he did not know a funereal atmosphere when he saw one, and it perplexed him. For moodiness on the part of James Piper he had been prepared, and he had not expected anything rollicking from his sister Florence, but Jeff and Vicky should surely have been more vivacious. Their gloom was as marked as that of Freddie had been when brooding on the mistaken liberality of the English dog owner. Vicky was pale and cold, and Jeff crumbled a good deal of bread.

At the conclusion of the meal there was a general move to the drawing-room, but Jeff went out on to the terrace, and Gally followed him there, eager for an explanation. When a man has gone all the way from Shropshire to London to further the interests of a young protégé, he resents it when the latter shows no appreciation of his efforts. It was with an offended rasp in his voice that he opened the conversation.

'Jeff,' he said, 'you look like the seven years of Famine we read of in Scripture. You could go on and play King Lear without make-up. Before going into the reasons for this – possibly you have been having another spell in the frigidaire with Florence – let me tell you a bit of news which ought to bring the sun smiling through. I saw Freddie; and I have headed him off.'

'You've done what?'

Gally could make nothing of the question. It bewildered him.

'Didn't Vicky tell you he was planning to come here?'

A spasm of pain contorted Jeff's face as if he were discovering too late that he had swallowed a bad oyster. His voice, when he replied, trembled.

'Vicky isn't speaking to me.'

'What do you mean, she isn't speaking to you? Got tonsillitis or something?'

'We've quarrelled.'

It was the last thing Gally was expecting, and he felt as a general might feel if his whole plan of campaign had been ruined by some eccentricity on the part of his troops. He had taken it for granted that, whatever else might go wrong, the love of his two clients could be relied on to remain unchanged.

'Quarrelled?' he gasped.

'Yes.'

'One of those lovers' tiffs?'

'Rather more than that, I'm afraid.'

'Big-time stuff?'

'Yes.'

'Your fault, of course?'

'I suppose so. She wanted me to elope with her, and I wouldn't.'

'Why not?'

'Because it would have meant letting Lord Emsworth down. He told me himself I was his last hope of getting the Empress painted. And another thing. What on earth would we have lived on? Unless Freddie sells that strip of mine. Did he say anything about that, by the way?'

Gally was grateful for the question. He had been wondering how to break the bad news.

'I'm afraid he did, my boy.'

That word 'afraid' could have only one meaning. Jeff gave a momentary quiver, and his mouth tightened, but he spoke calmly.

'Nothing doing?'

'Nothing.'

'About what I expected. It was very good of Freddie to bother himself with the job.'

His courageous bearing under the shattering blow increased Gally's already favourable opinion of Jeff. At Jeff's age he, like all Pelicans, had accepted impecuniosity as the natural way of life. If you had the stuff, you spent it; if you hadn't, you borrowed it. He had sometimes been best man at weddings where the proceedings were held up while the groom, short by fourteen shillings of the sum required of him, fumbled feverishly in his pockets, his only comment 'Well, this is a nice bit of box fruit, if you like.'

But Jeff, he knew, was different from the young Galahad. Jeff took life seriously. And very proper, too, the reformed Galahad felt.

'The future doesn't look rosy,' he said.

'Not excessively,' said Jeff.

'It's the old story – where's the money coming from?'

'That's it in a nutshell.'

'Isn't there anything you can do?'

'I'm a pretty good architect, but what good is that when I can't get commissions?'

'True. But first things first. We can't have you at outs with Vicky. I shall now proceed to sweeten her.'

'Fine, if you can do it. How do you propose to?'

'I shall tell her the tale,' said Gally.

Vicky was at the piano in the smaller drawing-room, playing old English folk songs, as girls will when their love life has gone awry. Gally's face was stern and his eye austere as he approached her. He was not pleased with her behaviour. Life, he considered, was difficult enough without girls giving excellent young men the pink slip and going off and playing old English folk songs.

'I've just been talking to Jeff,' he said, wasting no time with polite preliminaries. 'And don't sit there playing the piano at me,' he added, for this was what Vicky was continuing to do. 'He tells me you won't speak to him. Nice goings-on, I must say. He comes here, braving all the perils of Blandings Castle to be with you, and you give him the push. I can't follow your mental processes. Of course the fact of the matter is that you would now give anything if you could recall those cruel words.'

'What cruel words?'

'You know damn well what cruel words.'

'Must we discuss this?'

'It's what I came here to do.'

'You're wasting your time.'

'Oh, don't be a little idiot.'

'Thank you,' said Vicky, and she played a few bars of an old English folk song in a marked manner.

It occurred to Gally that he was allowing exasperation to interfere with his technique. Instead of telling the tale he was letting this tête-à-tête degenerate into a vulgar brawl. He hastened to repair his blunder.

'I'm sorry I called you an idiot.'

'Don't mention it.'

'I was not myself.'

'Who were you?'

Sticky going, Gally felt, extremely sticky going. The tale he told would have to be a good one. And fortunately his brain, working well, had come up with a pippin.

'The fact is,' he said, ignoring the question, which would not have been easy to answer, 'this unfortunate affair has woken old memories. There was a similar tragedy in my own life. Two loving hearts sundered owing to a foolish quarrel, and nothing to be done about it because we were both too proud to make the first move. It happened when I was a very young man and sadly lacking in sense. I loved a girl. I won't tell you her name. I will call her Deirdre.'

'I've often wondered how that name was spelled,' said Vicky meditatively. 'I suppose you start off with a capital D and then just trust to luck. Was she beautiful?'

'Beautiful indeed. Lovely chestnut hair, a superb figure and large melting eyes, in colour half way between a rook's egg and a bill stamp.[57] I loved her passionately, and it was my dearest wish to call her mine. But it was not to be.'

'Why wasn't it?'

'Because of my unfortunate sense of humour. She was the daughter of a bishop, very strict in her views.'

'And you told her one of your Pelican Club limericks?'

'No, not that. But I took her to dinner at a fashionable restaurant and thinking to amuse her I marched round the table with a soup plate on my head and a stick of celery in my hand, giving what I thought was a droll impersonation of a trooper of the Blues on guard at Whitehall. It was a little thing I had often done on Saturday nights at the Pelican to great applause, but she was deeply offended.'

'She thought you were blotto?'

'She did. And she swept out and married an underwriter at Lloyd's. I could have explained, but I was too proud.'

'Her cruel words had been too cruel?'

'Exactly.'

'How very sad.'

'I thought you would think so.'

'Though it would be a lot sadder if you hadn't told me that Dolly Henderson was the only woman you had ever wanted to marry. Deirdre must have slipped your memory.'

It was not easy to disconcert Gally. Not only his sisters Constance, Hermione and Florence, but dozens of bookmakers, policemen, three-card men and jellied eel sellers had tried to do it through the years and failed, but these simple words of Vicky's succeeded in doing so. As he stood polishing his eyeglass, for once in his life unable to speak, she continued her remarks.

'You certainly have nerve, Gally. The idea of trying to tell *me* the tale. One smiles.'

Gally was resilient. Not for him the shamefaced blush and the sheepish twiddling of the fingers. Recovering quickly from what had been an unpleasant shock, he spoke in a voice very different from his former melting tones.

'Oh, one does, does one?' he said. 'Well, one won't smile long. Listen to me, and I'm not telling the tale now. Jeff refused to sit in on your chuckleheaded idea of eloping for a very good reason.'

'He said he had to stay on and paint a pig.'

'That wasn't his only reason. He also didn't want to have to see you starving in the gutter. He had no job and no prospects and he knew that you had a good appetite and needed three squares a day.'[58]

'How absolutely absurd. I've all sorts of money.'

'Held in trust for you by your stepmother.'

'She'd have given it to me.'

'Want to bet?'

'Anyway we'd have got along somehow. There are a hundred things Jeff could have done.'

'Name three. I can only think of two – robbing a bank and stealing the Crown Jewels. The trouble with you, young Victoria, is that you're like all girls, you don't look ahead. You want something, and you go for it like a monkey after a banana. The more prudent male counts the cost.'

'When have you ever counted the cost?'

'Not often, I admit. But I'm not a prudent male. Jeff's different.'

There was a pause. Gally's voice had lacked the Sarah

Bernhardt note which had come into it when he had been telling the tale, but his words, even without that added attraction, were such as to give food for thought, and they had made Vicky look pensive. She played a bar or two with an abstracted air.

'I've thought of something,' she said suddenly.

'That's good. What?'

'There wouldn't be any need for us to starve in gutters. Freddie will sell that thing of Jeff's at any moment and we'll be all right even if I can't get my money. They pay millions for these comic strips in America, and they go on for ever. And when you're tired of doing the work yourself you hand it over to someone else and get paid just the same. Look at some of them. About as old as Blandings Castle, and I'll bet the fellows who started them have been dead for centuries.'

Gally saw that the time had come to acquaint this optimistic girl with the facts of life.

'I was about to touch on the J. Bennison comic strip,' he said. 'Don't expect a large annual income from it. Freddie tells me he has tried every possible market and nobody wants it. However promising an architect Jeff may have been, he apparently isn't good at comic strips. Don't blame him. Many illustrious artists would have had the same trouble. Michelangelo, Tintoretto and Holbein are names that spring to the mind.'

Gally's prediction that it would not be long before his niece ceased to smile was fulfilled with a promptitude which should have gratified him. If a bomb had exploded in the smaller drawing-room, scattering old English folk songs left and right, she could not have reacted more instantaneously. The haughtiness which had been so distasteful to her uncle fell from her like a garment.

'Oh, Gally!' she cried, her voice breaking and her attractive eyes widening to their fullest extent. 'Oh, the poor darling angel, he must be feeling *awful*.'

'He is,' said Gally, holding the view that this softer

mood should be encouraged. 'His reception of the news was pitiful to see. It knocked him flatter than a Dover sole. He reminded me of Blinky Bender, an old pal of mine at the Pelican, the time when he won sixty pounds on the fourth at Newmarket and suddenly realized that in order to collect the money he would have to go past five other bookies in whose debt he was. You had better run along and console him.'

'I will.'

'Making it clear that all is forgiven and forgotten and that you are sweethearts still,' said Gally, and he went off to get a glass of port in Beach's pantry.

I 2

Jeff had gone to his room after dinner and changed into a sweater and flannel trousers. There was a full moon, and it was his intention to sit on the terrace in its rays.[59] Not that he expected anything curative to come of this. He did not share Gally's confidence that telling the tale to Vicky would pick up the pieces of a shattered world and glue them together as good as new. He was aware that in his time Gally with his silver eloquence had played on hardened turf commissioners as on so many stringed instruments, but he could not but feel that the gifted man was faced now with a task beyond even his great powers. Those cruel words to which Gally had alluded in his conversation with Vicky were still green in Jeff's memory, and it was difficult to imagine a tale, however in the Sarah Bernhardt manner it might be told, persuading their speaker to consider them unsaid.

A knock on the door interrupted his sombre meditations, the different knock of one not sure of his welcome, and Lord Emsworth entered looking like a refugee from a three-alarm fire. He had removed the dress clothes which his sister Florence compelled him to don for dinner and put on the familiar baggy trousers and tattered shooting coat which few tramps would not have been too fastidious to appear in in public.

'Ah, Mr Smith,' he said, 'I hope I am not disturbing you.'

Jeff, though solitude was above all what he desired at the moment, assured him that he was not, and Lord Emsworth wandered to and fro, picking things up and dropping them, his habit when in a room new to him.

'I thought you might like to come and see the Empress by moonlight,' he said in the manner of someone inviting a friend to take a look at the Taj Mahal.

Six simultaneous things he would have preferred to do flashed through Jeff's mind, but consideration for a host of whom he had become very fond kept him from mentioning them and he replied that that would just make his day.

'But will she be up?' he asked, and Lord Emsworth asked up where.

'Won't she have gone to bed?'

'Oh, no, she always has a snack at about this hour.'

'Bran mash?'

'That and the other things prescribed by Wolfe-Lehmann.[60] According to Wolfe-Lehmann, whose advice I follow to the letter, a pig to be in health must consume daily nourishment amounting to fifty-seven hundred calories, these to consist of proteins four pounds seven ounces, carbohydrates twenty-five pounds.'

'It doesn't leave her much time for anything else.'

'No, she has few other interests.'

'Nothing like sticking to what you do best.'

'Exactly. We will go out by the back door and through the kitchen garden. It is the shortest way.'

The route indicated took them past Beach's pantry, and they could hear the butler's fruity laugh, indicating that Gally was telling him some humorous story from his deplorable youth. It surprised Jeff that anyone could laugh in the world as at present constituted. He himself was sunk in a gloom on which not even the prospect of seeing Empress of Blandings by moonlight could make an impression.

Lord Emsworth, on the other hand, was bright and chatty. He had returned to the subject of Sir Gregory Parsloe, on which he knew that his young friend would wish to be fully informed. It was not far to the Empress's sty, and the Parsloe saga provided absorbing, if one-sided, conversation all the way. If Jeff had had any doubts as to the depths of infamy to which baronets could sink,[61] they were resolved by the time he reached his destination. He did not suppose he would ever meet Sir Gregory Parsloe, but if he did he told himself he would be careful not to buy a used car from him.

At the sty Lord Emsworth paused.

'Have you a flask with you?' he asked.

'I beg your pardon?'

'A flask of whisky.'

This surprised Jeff. He had not suspected his host of being a drinking man, and in any case it seemed to him that the other might have quenched his thirst before leaving the house. He said he was sorry but he had not, and Lord Emsworth looked relieved.

'I asked because on one occasion somebody drank from a flask while at the rails of the sty and dropped it into the Empress's trough,[62] and I am sorry to say that she became completely intoxicated. My brother Galahad, I remember, suggested that she ought to join Alcoholics Anonymous, and I was very doubtful whether the committee would accept a pig. Fortunately we discovered the truth. But it was an anxious time.'

'It just shows you,' said Jeff.

'It does indeed,' said Lord Emsworth.

The Empress, as predicted, was having a late snack, and for what seemed to Jeff several hours they stood gazing at her. Eventually she appeared to feel that she had had sufficient to see her through till breakfast and retired to the covered portion of the sty, there to curl up and get the wholesome slumber which Wolfe-Lehmann no doubt considered essential to her health. Reluctantly Lord Emsworth led the way back to the house, and Jeff was privileged to hear how Sir Gregory Parsloe, stopping at nothing, had decoyed George Cyril Wellbeloved, Lord

Emsworth's superbly gifted pig man, from service at the castle to his own employment.

Entering through the back door, they separated, Lord Emsworth to proceed to his room and read Whiffle's *On the Care of the Pig*[63] for an hour or so before going to bed, Jeff to fulfil his original intention of sitting on the terrace in the moonlight.

It was soon after this that Gally bade Beach good night and Beach, having heard Lord Emsworth come in and remembering how often after these night expeditions he forgot to lock up, went to inspect the back door.

It was as he had thought. The door was not locked. He locked it.

Jeff, meanwhile, thankful to be alone, though naturally sorry that he was to hear no more about Sir Gregory Parsloe, continued to sit in the moonlight, smoking his pipe and looking on the dark side of things.

Jeff was one of those rare young men whose hearts, once bestowed, are bestowed for ever. In a world filled to overflowing with male butterflies flitting and sipping and then moving on to flit and sip somewhere else he remained as steadfast as Jacob or any of the others who became famous for their constancy. He had fallen in love with Vicky at their first meeting and he had been in love with her ever since, and the fact that he was now so low in her estimation made no difference to him. He had friends who in the same position, deprived of the girl they loved, would have consoled themselves with the thought that there would be another one along in a minute, but this easy philosophy was not for J. G. Bennison. The current situation made J. G. Bennison feel that hope was dead.

How long he would have sat there had nothing occurred to divert his thoughts, he could not have said, but one of the charms of the English climate is its ability to change from high summer to midwinter in a matter of minutes, and a bitter wind springing up from the east persuaded him that he would be more comfortable in bed.

It is rather saddening to think that his first emotion on reaching the back door and finding it locked was a surge of anti-Lord Emsworth feeling, for there was nothing to indicate that that absentminded peer was not responsible for the devastating act. Nothing could be truer to form than that his host should have locked up, completely forgetting that he had left a companion out on the terrace. Showing once again that in human affairs it is always the wrong man who gets the blame. Beach, who should have played the stellar role in Jeff's commination service, escaped without a curse.

Two courses were open to Jeff. He could ring bells and hammer on doors till he roused the house or he could stay outside for the night. Neither appealed to him. It was improbable that the first alternative would bring Lady Florence down in a dressing gown, but it was a possibility, and the thought of being pierced by those icy eyes was one that intimidated even a Smith who knew what fear was only by hearsay. On the other hand, with the wind freshening, remaining in the great outdoors offered few attractions.

It was as he stood there, this way and that dividing the swift mind, as somebody once put it, that he had a vague recollection, when on the terrace, of having seen an open window not very far above him, a window well within the reach of one who in his undergraduate days at Oxford had mastered the knack of climbing up walls and sliding through windows after lock-up. He had wondered whose it was.

Externally Blandings Castle might have been specially designed for the climber's convenience. Stout strands of ivy had been allowed to flourish on its walls till the merest novice would have experienced no difficulty in finding his way up.

A minute later he was window bound, glad to find that the old skill had not deserted him. Five minutes later he was across the sill. And twenty-five seconds after that the quiet night was disturbed by a noise like the shattering of a hundred dishes falling from the hands of a hundred waiters, and he was staggering across the floor with a bruised shin and drenched trouser legs. The occupant of the room, as he was to discover later, had placed beneath the window a jug full of water, several assorted fire irons, a chair, a picture of sheep in a meadow and another picture of a small girl nursing a kitten.

Lights flashed on, and a voice spoke, the voice of Claude Duff.

'Stick 'em up, or I shoot,' it said. 'It's all right shooting a burglar,' it added. 'I asked my solicitor.'[64]

13

That Jeff, climbing through the window in the dark, should have become entangled in fire irons, jugs of water and pictures of sheep and kittens was not surprising, for these had been stacked in close ranks, impossible to avoid. It was also less than extraordinary that he should have felt irritated with Claude Duff. A drier and less bruised man might have applauded Claude's prudence in consulting his solicitor before starting to take human life. Jeff felt only annoyance, and he expressed this in his opening words, which were:

'Oh, don't be a damned fool.'

'Jeff!' cried Claude in ringing tones, and Jeff snarled a reminder that danger lurked in addressing him thus. Who knew that Lady Florence was not even now with her hand on the door handle, all ready to join their little circle? The fire irons alone had made enough noise to wake a dozen Florences.

'I thought you were a burglar,' said Claude.

'Well, I'm not.'

'What *are* you exactly?' Claude asked. 'I mean, climbing up walls and sliding through windows. Conduct surely a bit on the eccentric side. No son of mine would do that sort of thing unless he were rehearsing for pantomime.'

'I was locked out by old Emsworth,' Jeff replied, though he should have said 'old Beach'. 'He took me out to see his pig by moonlight, and he forgot that I had gone on to the terrace. Tell me,' he went on more amiably, for the agony of his shin was now abating, 'What were those things doing on the floor?'

There was modest pride in Claude's voice as he answered the question.

'That was my own unaided idea. I can't sleep without a window open, so I always open one and set a booby-trap in case of burglars. I'm glad you turned out not to be one, for between you and me I was stretching the facts a bit when I said I was going to shoot. I haven't a gun.'

'But all right otherwise?'

'No complaints at all. I like it here. The slight crumpled rose leaf is that Piper's sister will be arriving at any moment. She's a terror.'

'She can't be worse than Florrie.'[65]

'My dear chap, she begins where the latter leaves off. Not that Lady Florence is a woman you would care to meet late at night down a dark alley. I was amazed when I thought she was Vicky's mother. Great relief when I found she was only step.'

'Vicky!'

The word had shot from Jeff's lips like a projectile.

'She asked me to call her Vicky.'

Jeff could not speak. He had not seen Claude Duff for some time, but he knew all about his uncanny gift for ensnaring the female heart. Women fell before him like ninepins and he was always falling before women. Not once but on several occasions Jeff had had to listen to outpourings from him reminiscent of the Song of Solomon. And Vicky, her eyes opened to the defects of J. G. Bennison, would be quite likely to fall under his spell, if she had not fallen already. Jeff had lost her, no argument about that, but that did not debar him from being shocked, horrified, appalled and rendered speechless by the prospect of her becoming another's.

Claude took advantage of his dumbness to proceed.

'I wouldn't say this to anyone except you, Jeff, but I'm in love. I've thought I was several times, I know, but this is the real thing. She was with Mr Threepwood when I arrived yesterday, and he introduced us. "This is my niece Miss Underwood," he said, and in a flash something told me I had met my ideal. It was the way she looked. You've probably not noticed, but she has a sort of sad expression, as if she had had some great sorrow in her life. One longs to pick her up and kiss her and comfort her. Do you believe in love at first sight, Jeff?'

Long association with Claude had given Jeff plenty of opportunity of making up his mind about this phenomenon, even if he had not had his own experience to guide him, but still unable to speak, he answered neither in the affirmative or the negative, and Claude continued.

'It's an odd thing that this should have happened, because up till now I've always been attracted by tallish girls, and Vicky's so small and dainty. What are those statuette things you hear people talking about? Tan something.'

Jeff was apparently unable to help him, for he remained silent.

'Tan?' said Claude, snapping his fingers. 'Tan? Tan? Tanagra,' he said, inspired. 'She's a Tanagra statuette.[66] I've never seen one, but I know what they must be like. Jeff, old man, do you think I have a chance. She's not engaged to anybody, is she?'

'No,' said Jeff, speaking for the first time. It was a point on which he was well informed.

'Then I may have a chance. Do you think I have a chance, Jeff? We got along like a couple of sailors on shore leave, and fortunately money is no problem. A secretary doesn't make a fortune, though I hope you'll stick old Emsworth for a packet when and if, but I can lay my hands on something better any time I want to. One of my uncles is Duff of Duff and Trotter, and he's always after me to go into the business. I've held off so far because of the prestige of being with Piper, but now that I plan to get married . . .'

Jeff could bear no more.

'Good night,' he said.

'But, Jeff, don't go yet, old man.'

'Good *night*,' said Jeff.

It was with heart bowed down that he sought the seclusion of his bedroom. He had supposed it already bowed down about as far as it could go, but he realized now that he had underestimated its capabilities for sinking. There is a difference, subtle but well-marked, between the emotions of a lover who has been told by the girl he loves that all is over between them and those of a lover who, tottering from this blow, sees a Claude Duff beginning to exercise his fascinations on her. In the former case he has a hope, if only a weak one; in the latter, merely despair.

Jeff was a modest man and could think clearly, and he was miserably conscious that between himself and a charmer like Claude Duff there could be no contest. Take looks, for instance. They ought not to count, but they do. And he was what dramatic critics call adequate. Claude was spectacular.

Claude could play the piano, always a gift of maximum assistance to a wooer. And in addition to this he had only to fall in with his uncle's wishes to have plenty of money at his disposal. It was ridiculous to hope to compete with a man so armed at every point.

With Jeff so sunk in the slough of despond it might have seemed that nothing could bring him even momentarily to the surface; but that this feat could be accomplished was proved before he had gone the length of the corridor. All that was needed was for someone to steal up behind him, tap him on the shoulder and say 'Ho'. Sergeant Murchison, appearing from nowhere, did this, and Jeff came out of his thoughts with a start which could not have been more violent if, like Lord Emsworth's pig man, he had seen the White Lady of Blandings.

14

The trouble about being the chronicler of a place like Blandings Castle, where someone is always up to something and those who are not up to something are up to something else, is that you have so many people to write about that you tend to push quite deserving characters into the background. Sergeant Murchison is a case in point. Mention, it is true, has been made of him from time to time, but only casual mention. Not a word has been said of the way he felt about things, not a syllable concerning his love for Marilyn Poole, Lady Diana's maid, and the public is left without a clue as to whether he liked his daily duties or disliked them.

Now it can be told. His daily duties gave him the heeby-jeebies. In jaundiced mood he regarded himself as a bird in a gilded cage. It was as distasteful to him to have to follow Sir James Piper wherever he went as it was to Sir James to be followed. Often he thought wistfully of the brave old days when he had been a simple constable walking a beat in Whitechapel or Bottleton East[67] with platoons of drunks and disorderlies on every side, inviting him to make a pinch. Where, he asked himself bitterly, were those pinches now? Gone with the wind, one with Nineveh and Tyre.

It can be readily appreciated, therefore, that when, smoking at his window and thinking of Marilyn and her distressing habit of flirting with Sir James's chauffeur, he saw a sinister figure climbing up the castle wall, he had felt as the poet Wordsworth used to do when he beheld a rainbow in the sky. (Wordsworth's heart, it will be remembered, always leaped up when this happened.) To race downstairs would have been with him the work of an instant if he had not slowed himself up by tripping over a loose mat.

However, the marauder was still there when he reached the corridor, so he crept up behind him, tapped him on the shoulder and said 'Ho'.

The effect of this on Jeff was electrical. To have hands tapping him on the shoulder and voices saying 'Ho' where no hands or voices should have been would have startled the most phlegmatic man. He rose perhaps six inches into the air and came to earth too short of breath to speak. Sergeant Murchison took it on himself to keep the conversation going.

'You're pinched,' he said.

'Pinched!' said Jeff, recovering enough breath for the simple monosyllable.

'Pinched,' said Sergeant Murchison, and would have spelled the word if so desired.

This completed Jeff's illusion of having lost his reason. Oh, what a noble mind is here o'erthrown, he might have said to himself if he had remembered the quotation. All he could find to say was a feeble 'How do you mean pinched?' and Sergeant Murchison said he meant pinched.

'Who are you?' Jeff asked. It is always well to know the identity of the officer pinching us.

'Sergeant E. B. Murchison, special representative of Scotland Yard. And I'm taking you to Lord Emsworth, who will decide what's to be done with you.'

And so it came about that Lord Emsworth, deep in Whiffle's *On the Care of the Pig*, was wrenched from its magic pages by the entry of two intruders, one young Smith, whom he had come to love as a son, the other someone he did not remember having seen before. However, any friend of his friend Smith was a friend of his, and he liked the affectionate way the man was holding on to Smith's arm, so he welcomed the pair warmly.

'Come in, my dear Smith, come in Mr er, er. I'm sorry, I keep forgetting your name. You know how one does.'

'Murchison, m'lord.'

'Of course. Murchison. Quite.'

'Of Scotland Yard.'

This puzzled Lord Emsworth.

'But that's in London, isn't it?'

'Yes, m'lord.'

'Then what are you doing in Shropshire?'

Jeff was able to answer this.

'He's arresting me.'

'Doing what?'

'Arresting me.'

'Why?'

'For making a burglarious entry,' said Sergeant Murchison.

Something stirred in Lord Emsworth. His memory might be poor where recent events were concerned, but it was excellent about things that had happened thirty years ago, especially if these were of no importance whatsoever.

'Bless my soul,' he said, 'that reminds me of a song in a musical comedy Galahad took me to when we were young men. About the Grenadier Guards guarding the Bank of England at night. How did it go? "If you've money or plate in the bank," sang Lord Emsworth in a reedy tenor like an escape of gas, "we're the principal parties to thank. Our regiment sends you a squad that defends you from anarchists greedy and lank." '

'M'lord,' said Sergeant Murchison.

' "In the cellars and over the roof," ' continued Lord Emsworth, who was not an easy man to stop, ' "we keep all intruders aloof, and no-one can go in to rob Mr Bowen of what he describes as the oof." Bowen must

87

have been the manager of the Bank of England at that time, don't you think?'

'M'lord,' said Sergeant Murchison.

' "That's our right. And if any wicked gentry try by night to make a burglarious entry, they take fright at the sight of the busbied sentry." '[68]

'M'lord,' said Sergeant Murchison, 'this man was climbing up the castle wall and getting in at one of the windows.'

'I was locked out,' said Jeff.

'Very sensible of you to climb up the wall, then.'

'I didn't like to rouse the house.'

'Very considerate of you. Different from Baxter, a former secretary of mine. He was locked out one night and he threw flower pots in at my window. A most unpleasant experience to be asleep in bed and have the air suddenly become thick with flower pots.[69] A flower pot can give you a nasty bruise. But how, my dear Mr Murchison,' said Lord Emsworth, reasoning closely, 'can Smith have been making a burglarious entry when he's staying here?'

'He's staying here?' Scotland Yard trains its sons well. They remain unmoved under the worst of shocks. Sergeant Murchison had seldom received a more disintegrating blow, but he did not so much as totter. 'You know him?'

'He is the artist who is painting the portrait of my pig.'

Sergeant Murchison was a man who could face facts. He did not need further evidence to tell him that the pinch of which he had thought so highly had been but a mirage. He turned and left the room.

'I don't much like your friend Murchison,' said Lord Emsworth, as the door closed. 'He reminds me of my sister Constance. The same look on his face, as if he suspected everybody he met. Constance is now in America. You are not American, are you?'

'No.'

'I thought you might be. So many people are nowadays. Constance married an American. I went out there for the wedding. Do you know that in America they give you boiled eggs mashed up in a glass?'[70]

'Really?'

'I assure you. It takes away all the fun of eating a boiled egg. A most interesting country, though. Galahad used to go there a great deal at one time. Galahad was always the adventurous type. Peanut butter.'

'I beg your pardon?'

'It is much eaten in America. I was told that you put jam on it. If you like jam, of course. And after they have finished eating peanut butter they go out and contact people and have conferences. Which reminds me. That step-daughter of my sister Florence's, I forget her name but you have probably met her, nice girl, she often gives the Empress a potato, she is trying to contact you. I met her roaming about the place and she asked me if I had seen you, because it was most important that you and she should have a conference. You're not leaving me, are you, my dear fellow?'

Jeff was leaving him. He was already at the door. Hope, so recently consigned to the obituary column, had cast off its winding cloths and risen from the grave. Lord Emsworth might see nothing sensational in the fact that Vicky was roaming about the place trying to confer with him, but to Jeff it was so significant that the world suddenly became a thing of joy and laughter and even Lord Emsworth in his old shooting coat and baggy trousers seemed almost beautiful.

Girls, he knew, changed their minds. They thought things over and reversed decisions. The girl who on Monday hissed that she never wanted to see you again was quite likely to be all smiles and affection on Tuesday – or at the latest at some early hour on Wednesday.

It came, accordingly, as no surprise to him when he met Vicky not far from Lord Emsworth's door and she flung herself into his arms with the words 'Oh, Jeff, darling!' They stood locked together, the past forgotten, and Lord Emsworth, coming out of his room, eyed them with paternal benevolence.

Lord Emsworth had come out of his room because he hoped that Jeff was still within reach. He wanted to discuss with him the question, which they had omitted to touch on, of whether Jeff should depict the Empress full face or in profile. He refrained from bringing this up at a moment when the young fellow's mind was so obviously on other things, so he went back into his room and sat there for some time plunged in thought.

The result of his thoughts was to send him to the room of his sister Florence.

'Oh, Florence,' he said, 'could I have a word with you?'

'I hope it is important, Clarence. I was asleep.'

'It is. Very important. Do you remember coming to me some time ago and kicking up no end of a row because your step-daughter was in love with a fellow named Bennison?'

'I remember mentioning it,' said Florence with dignity. She disliked his choice of phrases.

'Well, you can make your mind easy. She isn't in love with Bennison at all. The chap she loves is my friend Smith. I saw them just now hugging and kissing like the dickens.'

15

Florence may have been asleep at the moment when Lord Emsworth knocked on her door, but she was wide awake now. It was her practice to put mud on her face before retiring to rest, and such was her emotion as he delivered what a gossip column writer would have called his exclusive that this mud cracked from side to side like the mirror of Tennyson's Lady of Shalott.

'Is this a joke, Clarence?' she demanded, directing at him a look lower in temperature even than those which Jeff had had to face on his arrival. 'Are you trying to be funny?'

'Certainly not,' said Lord Emsworth indignantly. He had not tried to be funny since the remote days of school, when it had taken the form of pulling a chair away from a friend who was about to sit down. 'I tell you I saw them. I came out of my room and there they were, as close together as the paper on the wall. I was delighted, of course.'

'Delighted?'

'Naturally. I knew how greatly you objected to the chap you thought Victoria was in love with, and what could be better than that she should have had second thoughts while there was still time and taken up with my friend Smith, a charming fellow thoroughly sound on pigs?'

'And a penniless artist who has to take any tuppenny job that's offered to him.'

'If you consider painting the portrait of Empress of Blandings a tuppenny job, I disagree with you,' said Lord Emsworth with dignity. 'And he isn't a penniless artist.

Galahad tells me he is very well off, and only paints pigs because he loves them.'

At the sound of that name Florence started so violently that more mud fell from her face. Experience had taught her that no good could ever come of anything with which Galahad was connected. She began to feel like the man in the poem who on a lonely road did walk in fear and dread and having once looked back walked on and turned no more his head, because he knew a frightful fiend did close behind him tread. Galahad and frightful fiends, not much to choose between them. She was normally a pale woman, as any woman with a brother like that had a right to be, but now she turned scarlet.

'Galahad!' she cried.

'Smith's a friend of his. It was he who arranged for him to come to the castle. I had been trying with no success to get Royal Academicians and people like that to paint the Empress, but Galahad said No, what I wanted was an eager young enthusiastic chap like Smith. So he sounded him about coming here, and fortunately he was at liberty. So he came. But I mustn't keep you up. You're anxious to turn in. Is that mud you've got on your face? How very peculiar. I always say you never know what women will be up to next. Well, good night, Florence, good night,' said Lord Emsworth, and he trotted off to renew his interrupted study of Whiffle.

If he had supposed that on his departure Florence would curl up and go to sleep, he erred. Late though the hour was, nothing was further from her thoughts than slumber. She sat in a chair, her powerful brain working like a dynamo.

It was of Galahad that she was thinking. It seemed incredible that even he could have had the audacity to introduce into Blandings Castle the infamous Bennison at the thought of whom she had been shuddering for weeks, but he might well have done so. Long association with him had told her that the slogan that ruled his life was Anything Goes.

16

Brenda Piper, one of those hardy women who do not mind getting up early, caught the 8.30 express to Market Blandings on the following morning, and Jno Robinson took her to the castle in his taxi.

The last time Jno and his taxi appeared in this chronicle was when he had Gally as a passenger and then, it will be remembered, there was a complete fusion of soul between employer and employed and the most delightful harmony prevailed. It was very different on this occasion. Briefness of acquaintance never deterred Brenda from becoming personal and speaking her mind. If in her opinion someone she had only just met required criticism, criticism was what he got.

Jno Robinson had not yet shaved. She mentioned this. His costume was informal, of the Lord Emsworth school rather than that of Beau Brummell. This too, was touched on. She also thought poorly of his skill as a driver, and said so. The result was that when they drew up at the front door of Blandings Castle it needed only the discovery that she did not approve of tipping to round out the ruin of Jno Robinson's day.

Before going in search of her brother James, Brenda presented herself to her hostess and was concerned to see how pale she was. Florence, as has been indicated, had slept badly.

'Good gracious,' she exclaimed. 'What ever is the matter, Florence? Are you ill? If it's a cold coming on, take two aspirins and go to bed.'

Florence shook her head. It was not medical advice she needed.

'I had a bad night, but I'm perfectly well. It's Victoria. You know the trouble I am having with her. That man of hers.'

'Surely not now that she is at the castle?'

'But he is here, too.'

'*Here*?'

'Galahad sneaked him in. Clarence wanted someone to paint his pig, and Galahad produced this man.'

'You're sure he's the one?'

'Quite sure.'

'Then –'

'Why don't I turn him out? Because I have no proof. You know how often you hear that the police are certain that somebody has done some crime, but they cannot make an arrest until they have proof. It's the same here.'

'I'd kick him out and chance it.'

'It would mean trouble with Clarence. Of course if I had proof there would be no difficulty. Even Clarence could not object then.'

Privately Brenda did not attach much importance to any possible objections on Lord Emsworth's part, but she abstained from her customary candour because she was thinking. The trend of her thoughts became evident a moment later.

'I know what you can do,' she said. 'Didn't you tell me that Victoria told you that this man Bennison had been employed as a drawing instructor at Daphne Winkworth's school? Well, ring up Daphne and get a description of him.'

'I'll do it at once,' said Florence. She felt that one could always rely on Brenda.

She hastened to the telephone.

'Daphne.'

'Who is this?'

'Florence.'

'Oh, how are you, Florence dear?'

'Very worried. I rang up to ask you to do something for me.'

'Anything, of course.'

'It's just to describe a man named Bennison.'

'Do you mean who used to be here as drawing master?'

'Used to be! Aha!'

'Why do you say Aha?'

'Because I suspect Galahad of having sneaked him into Blandings under a false name.'

'Galahad is capable of anything.'

'Anything.'

'I won't enquire as to his motives. Being Galahad – one can assume that they were bad . . .'

'They were.'

'Well, Mr Bennison is about five foot eleven, well built, clean shaven, fair hair, and he has a small scar just under his right eye. A football accident, I believe. I wouldn't say for certain that his nose hadn't been broken at some time. Does this meet your requirements?

'It does,' said Florence. 'It does indeed. Thank you, Daphne. I am very grateful to you.'

Armed with this information, she went out into the grounds in search of Gally. She found him in the hammock under the cedar and for once took no offence at his occupancy of it. A sister about to bathe a brother in confusion and, though she could not count on this, bring the blush of shame to his cheek, has no time to bother about hammocks.

She was all amiability as she opened her attack.

'Having a little sleep, Galahad?'

'Not at the moment. Thinking deep thoughts.'

'About what?'

'Oh, this and that.'

'Cabbages and kings?'

'That sort of thing.'

'Did you meditate at all on Mr Smith?'

'Not that I remember.'

'I thought you might have been wondering why he called himself that.'

'Why shouldn't he? It's his name.'

'Really? I always thought his name was Bennison.'

Gally's training at the old Pelican Club stood him in good stead. Membership at that raffish institution always equipped a man with the ability to remain outwardly calm under the impact of nasty surprises. Somebody like Fruity Biffen, taken aback when his Assyrian beard fell off, might register momentary dismay, but most members beneath the slings and arrows of outrageous fortune were able to preserve the easy nonchalance of a Red Indian at the stake. Gally did so now. Nobody could have told that he was feeling as though a charge of trinitrotoluol had been touched off under him. His frank open face showed merely the bewilderment of a brother who was at a loss to know what his sister was talking about.

'Why on earth should you think his name was Bennison?'

'Because last night Clarence saw him hugging and kissing Victoria. It seemed to me odd behaviour if they had only known each other about twenty-four hours.'

Gally was astounded.

'He was kissing her?'

'Yes.'

'You accept Clarence's unsupported word?'

'Yes.'

'You don't think he was having one of those hallucinations people have?'

'I do not.'

'I knew a chap at the Pelican who thought he was being followed about by a little man with a black beard. Well, I will certainly speak to Smith about this. But I still think Clarence must have been mistaken.'

'Have you known him long?'

'Ages. We grew up together.'

'You did what?'

'Oh, you mean Smith. I thought you meant Clarence. Yes, I've known Smith quite a while. Not so long as I've known Clarence, of course, but long enough to be sure he's just the man Vicky ought to marry.'

'And I'm sure that his name is Bennison and that you brought him to the castle.'

Gally shook his head reproachfully. He was not angry, but you could see he was terribly hurt.

'You ought not to say such things, Florence. You have wounded me deeply.'

'Good.'

'You have caused me great pain.'

'You'll distribute it.'

'What beats me is where you got this preposterous notion.'

'I ought to have told you that. From my friend Daphne Winkworth, at whose school Mr Bennison was employed for quite a time. She gave me a most accurate description of him, down to the scar you will have noticed under his right eye. Well, I think that is all, Galahad, and you may go back to your deep thinking. I have of course told Victoria that Mr Bennison is leaving the castle immediately.'

Notes

1. Since the Chancellor of the Exchequer holds his office for the whole of Great Britain and Northern Ireland, we may expect that the shorthand reference to 'England' would have been amended by Wodehouse or his editor to 'Britain'. It is an example of the sort of minor error into which he fell through prolonged absence from England, several examples of which can be found in his draft of this book.

2. This makes the ninth recorded sister of Clarence and Galahad, with one more to check in (see note 5).

3. Wodehouse, generally through the voice of Galahad, often called Blandings Castle a Bastille, sometimes Devil's Island.

4. Would a Scotland Yard detective call the Chancellor of the Exchequer 'Sir James'? Richard Usborne is strongly of the view that he would have said 'Sir', and that this is another example of what the author had forgotten during his absence from the country. He points out that the words 'somber', 'behavior', 'demeanor', etc., can be found in the typescript although Wodehouse would not have spelt them that way in a letter to England. The typescripts of his books went first to his American agent for duplication and sending out to publishers. His English publishers would make the alterations of spelling for the English market. Richard had an early English edition of *Leave it to Psmith* in which 'arbor' and 'arbour' can be found in different chapters.

5. Lady Diana Phipps, née Threepwood, completes the roll-call of Threepwood sisters. Wodehouse had a pleasant devil-may-care attitude to the species, and on page 4 Gally only mentions four of the ten, including the newcomer Diana. Nine times out of ten his purpose in dragging in sisters is to provide 'heavies', people to act as hostess at the Castle, boss Lord Emsworth, disapprove of Gally and say 'No' to lovers of daughters and nieces. Lady Florence and Lady Diana have never been

mentioned before, and for the first time the benevolent author has given us a sister we can like, even though she says nothing and doesn't even come on stage.

The final roster of sisters is therefore:

Lady Ann Warblington	*Something Fresh*
Lady Charlotte	'The Crime Wave at Blandings'
Lady Constance Keeble (later Schoonmaker)	*Leave it to Psmith*, *Summer Lightning*, *Heavy Weather*, *Pigs Have Wings*, *Service with a Smile*, *Galahad at Blandings*, *A Pelican at Blandings*, 'The Crime Wave at Blandings', 'Lord Emsworth and the Girl Friend', 'Sticky Wicket at Blandings'
Georgiana, Marchioness of Alcester	'Company for Gertrude', 'The Go-Getter'
Lady Hermione Wedge	*Full Moon*, *Pigs Have Wings*
Lady Dora Garland	*Full Moon*, *Pigs Have Wings*
Lady Julia Fish	*Summer Lightning*, *Heavy Weather*
Lady Jane (probably Allsop)	'Pig-Hoo-o-o-o-ey'
Lady Florence Moresby (formerly Underwood)	*Sunset at Blandings*
Lady Diana Phipps	*Sunset at Blandings*

Apart from Clarence and Gally there was one additional brother, now deceased. The late Lancelot Threepwood made a brief offstage appearance in *Summer Lightning*.

Galahad disliked all his sisters other than Diana and said to Clarence in *Galahad at Blandings*: 'I've always said it was a mistake to have sisters. We should have set out faces against them from the outset.'

The family tree of the Eighth Earl of Emsworth can be found on pages 116 and 117.

6. The fact that Lady Diana's first husband was (a) handsome and (b) named Rollo makes one sure that she was lucky that he was eaten by a lion. In Wodehouse, as a general rule, all male Christian names ending in 'o', such as Cosmo, Orlo, Orlando and Rollo (though not nicknames, such as Pongo, Boko, Bimbo or Bingo) stamped a man as being a wet, a sponger or a fool. Hugo, as in Hugo Carmody, is the only acceptable male

Christian name with an 'o' at the end. As though to emphasize this, when the short golf story 'The Long Hole', which first appeared in *Strand* in August 1921, appeared in the American magazine *McClure's* in March 1922, the name Ralph Bingham had been changed to Rollo Bingham, and both these names were carried through to book publication in the respective countries.

7. Wodehouse's best girls (such as Stiffy Byng, Nobby Hopwood and Bobbie Wickham) certainly dominated their loved ones (respectively, the Rev 'Stinker' Pinker, 'Boko' Fittleworth and 'Kipper' Herring). It looks as though this last novel might have almost amounted to a reverse message to all mankind: 'Dominate her. She'll love it, and you.'

Another major character in the Blandings novels (and elsewhere) was Lord Ickenham, a frequent adviser (generally unasked) of timid young men. His advice was the same: 'Go to the girl you have been nervously and distantly adoring, grab her like a sack of coals, waggle her about a bit, shower kisses on her upturned face and murmur passionate words (e.g. 'My mate') into her ear. This seldom fails.'

One wonders what percentage of girls would react today by calling for the nearest policeman. The approach got Cyril McMurdo, himself an ardent copper, a slap on the face from old Nannie Byles the first time he tried it on in *Cocktail Time*, but it brought good results in the end.

There are many other examples in Wodehouse of the worm turning, not just in Blandings stories (although Lord Emsworth himself succeeded on several occasions, e.g. over McAllister, when hand-in-hand with the Girl Friend; over his sister Constance and Baxter in the matter of an airgun; and over Daphne Winkworth after the Empress bit her son). Bertie Wooster was enabled to dominate his Aunt Agatha and Spode, with Jeeves's help, though it was invariably a false dawn when he thought he could dominate Jeeves or one of his ex-fiancées. Jeeves advised many of his clients (Oliver Sipperley, Gussie Fink-Nottle) to try to dominate their paramours. Lord Marshmoreton, like Lord Emsworth, was plagued by a bossy sister, and took the dramatic step of introducing a new young wife as his way of achieving domination.

8. Following on from note 7, we may assume that Florence will

be reconciled to her weak husband but, equally surely, only when she has seen him rise and dominate someone – herself, one hopes. Lord Emsworth achieves good results when (Scenario, chapter 21) he rises and dominates Florence and her hanger-on, Brenda, for such is their surprise and annoyance that they leave the Castle.

9. The Pelican Club, in Denman Street, Soho, was short-lived (1887–92), but fondly remembered: by Galahad, who had been a prominent member; by Arthur Binstead, in books such as *A Pink 'Un and a Pelican* and *Pitcher in Paradise*; and by J. B. Booth in *Old Pink 'Un Days*. For an authoritative analysis of the links between the Pelican and the Drones see *In Search of Blandings* by N. T. P. Murphy, and for some relevant tales see his imaginative book *The Reminiscences of Galahad Threepwood*.

10. Jno Robinson has been the owner-driver of the Market Blandings station taxi since *Heavy Weather*.

11. Millicent Threepwood said this at the start of *Summer Lightning*, and it was recalled, unattributed, in *Galahad at Blandings*, chapter 3.

12. This paragraph is repeated, almost word for word, from *Galahad at Blandings*, chapter 2, although the end of the last sentence, concerning Gally's policemen friends, is new.

13. Beach had been butler at the Castle since the first book, *Something Fresh*, when he had an under-butler, Merridew. In the short story 'Lord Emsworth Acts for the Best', when he had decided to resign in protest against his Lordship's beard, we learned that he had been at the Castle for eighteen years, starting as under-footman. Eighteen years it remained, through all the subsequent novels, for Wodehouse never treated time with anything other than irreverence.

However, time does not quite stand still for Gally, for he says for the first time that he is fed up with London. We have always before seen Galahad as a deep-dyed Londoner, seldom far from the bars and barmaids, theatres and clubs of the West End – essentially a visitor to, rather than resident at, Blandings. In *Full Moon* he said that he had never been able to understand his brother's objections to London, a city which he himself had always found an earthly paradise. Now it seems that, although he maintains rooms in London, he had come to look on his family home (despite the presence of sisters on the premises and Sir Gregory Parsloe-Parsloe across the fields) 'as near resembling an enchanted fairyland as dammit'.

14. When Beach was suborned in his pantry by Ronnie Fish to help him steal the Empress of Blandings in *Summer Lightning*, chapter 3, he put a green baize cover over the bullfinch's cage lest it should be shocked by what it heard. Since the average life of a caged bullfinch is around twelve years, it can be reasonably assumed that it was the same bird which provided companionship to Beach in each of the two books.

15. Clearly this means that the action of *Sunset at Blandings* follows that of *A Pelican at Blandings* by a week. *Heavy Weather* had followed *Summer Lightning* by a fortnight, and *Pigs Have Wings* was a year later.

16. Galahad's monocle was a flexible tool which freely expressed its personality whenever its owner suffered a shock or a surprise. In *Galahad at Blandings* he wore it in his right eye; in *A Pelican at Blandings* in his left.

17. This is the start of an interesting attribution of family status. Vicky is Galahad's sister Florence's step-daughter, whom Florence inherited when marrying her first husband, J. B. Underwood. The fact that Gally 'always enjoyed her company' suggests that he had known her for many years, and therefore that Florence's marriage had been some considerable time ago. The courtesy title 'niece' evidently came naturally.

18. According to Norman Murphy, the Gardenia Club in Leicester Square was one of many started when the Licensing Acts of the 1870s required restaurants to close at 12.30 a.m. The Gardenia was a dancing club and unusually had both female and male members. It was opened, probably in 1882, by the Bohee brothers, black musicians who had come from America with Haverley's Minstrels. They sold the club to William Dudley Ward, father of the MP for Southampton, 1906–22. Dudley Ward persuaded La Goulue (see Toulouse Lautrec's *Moulin Rouge* drawings) to appear at the club. He sold the club to an Australian, 'Shut-Eye' Smith, who owned it when the police closed it down in about 1889, probably for infringement of the drinking rules.

19. Augustus Whipple was stated to be a member of the

Athenæum Club in *Galahad at Blandings* and General Willoughby was known to give lunch there to Egbert Wedge. It was not the sort of place that would have attracted Gally, however, and Wodehouse succinctly pointed out the character of its members in *Sam the Sudden*, chapter 5:

> The interruption appeared to come on the three debaters like a bombshell. It had on them an effect much the same as an uninvited opinion from a young and newly joined member would have on a group of bishops and generals in the smoking-room of the Athenæum Club.

20. Wodehouse had scored out a last sentence to this first paragraph of the chapter. It read: 'And this had always struck him as odd, for his sister Florence, her mother, had even in childhood been constructed of aristocratic ice.' He presumably omitted it because Florence was Vicky's step-mother, not her real mother, but the expression 'constructed of aristocratic ice' is too good a nifty to lose entirely.

21. 'Mariana at the Moated Grange' was a favourite Wodehouse allusion, and can be found *inter alia* in *Full Moon*, chapter 5, and *Pigs Have Wings*, chapter 4.

22. Dolly Henderson married Jack Cotterleigh of the Irish Guards, and their delightful daughter (Sue Brown was her stage name) married Ronnie Fish, son of Galahad's sister Julia (*Summer Lightning* and *Heavy Weather*).

23. It is only in *A Pelican at Blandings* and this novel that the Eighth Earl of Emsworth, father of Clarence, Galahad, Lancelot and ten daughters, gets more than a line. It is odd that the benign Wodehouse dragged the eighth earl from his grave to make a rather nasty character of him, here a 'bully and a tyrant', and generally rather an ogre. Although we do not know how long ago Clarence succeeded to the title, we know that his father was seventy-seven when he was killed in the hunting-field, that Beach has served the ninth earl for eighteen years, that the ninth earl was the eldest of his father's thirteen children and that Vicky Underwood can just remember the eighth earl as someone who terrified her.

24. Jeff Bennison is not the only inappropriate suitor to have been reduced to teaching in a girls' school. In *Galahad at Blandings* Wilfred Allsop had been employed as piano teacher

by Dame Daphne Winkworth until her son exposed Jeff's use of an occasional drink to stiffen the nerves.

25. See *Full Moon* and *Galahad at Blandings*.

26. Lord Emsworth never did manage to get his beloved Empress painted for the Portrait Gallery at the Castle. This quest was a strong strand in the plot of *Full Moon* and there, too, the portrait painter, Bill Lister, came in under an assumed name, Messmore Breamworthy. After Bill had been ejected for experimenting in the cubist form and making the Empress appear both oblong and tight, he returned at Gally's instigation with a beard, the name Landseer, and the reputation of having painted *The Pig at Bée* – Bée being a village in the Swiss Alps.

27. Connie was still on the Atlantic Ocean at the end of *A Pelican at Blandings*, and had clearly left the Castle not more than two weeks before the start of this novel. Are we really expected to believe that a secretary-less Lord Emsworth would have stirred himself sufficiently to obtain the names and addresses of a series of prominent artists, to have approached them and to have been rejected by them, all in the space of about ten days? This may have required a little attention on a later draft, and perhaps the simplest solution would be to have delayed the action of this book by two or three weeks.

28. Around 1970 Wodehouse himself appeared in wax at Madame Tussaud's in London, but was not positioned, as far as is known, in the Chamber of Horrors.

29. The idea that Eastbourne (where Beach's mother lived) is on the east coast is another of the points of detail which should have been picked up by the author or editor prior to publication. Eastbourne is of course on the south coast, in East Sussex, some sixty-two miles east of the town of Emsworth on the West Sussex/Hampshire border.

30. In this novel Dame Daphne Winkworth does not come nearer than being an off-stage employer who relieves Jeff Bennison of his position, and later describes his appearance on the telephone to Florence. This is sufficient to puncture Jeff's alias at Blandings.

Dame Daphne, who appeared in *The Mating Season* and *Galahad at Blandings*, is one of the few links (Sir Roderick Glossop, the loony-doctor, is another) between the worlds of Bertie Wooster and Lord Emsworth. In *The Mating Season* she 'used to be headmistress of a big girls' school', but in her two Blandings appearances she *is* a headmistress. One assumes that she was an early advocate of the now ubiquitous career break for professional women, staying at home for a few years until her son Huxley became so obnoxious that he had to be sent to public school, at which point she may have moved back into the industry as proprietress of her Eastbourne jailhouse.

31. See *Galahad at Blandings*.

32. After their chance meeting which ended so cordially, Claude Duff and Gally seem to have separated. We would surely have been told how by the time the final draft had been completed.

33. When this story was told in *Full Moon*, chapter 3, and *A Pelican at Blandings*, chapter 4, Fruity Biffen was trying to avoid bookmakers at Hurst Park. It may be hoped that an assiduous editor would have run a check on this point.

34. Richard Usborne was informed by Fortnum & Mason (which he always supposed to be Wodehouse's recurrent 'Duff & Trotter') as to how a raised pie is made. Pastry, lightly cooked, is moulded round, or raised up, a wooden mould. The mould is then removed, the pastry filled with meat (usually game or pork) and the contents closed over with pastry again. The pie is then baked and served cold after a savoury jelly has been poured into the top to surround and seal off the meat.

35. The second son of Lord Emsworth, and originally a sore trial to his father. In 'The Custody of the Pumpkin' he married Aggie Donaldson, the daughter of an American millionaire and 'a sort of cousin' of Angus McAllister, the Blandings gardener.

Freddie rose to great heights in his father-in-law's dog-biscuit business and his father was glad to have him successful, married and several thousand miles away from the Castle.

36. Hermione Wedge was indeed a Threepwood sister, but it seems likely that the reference would have been changed to Florence in a later draft.

37. 'Blandings Castle has impostors like other houses have mice,' said Gally on one occasion, and the total count reached twenty with Jeff's appearance. To arrive at this total it is necessary to include Baxter on the occasion that he appeared under his own name at the instigation of Lady Constance, in

order to undertake a criminal act. It also includes Vanessa Polk
who, whilst actually being Vanessa Polk, was not the daughter
of the same Mr Polk that she had led Constance to believe
when she was wangling her invitation to the Castle. But, as it
did not take place at the Castle, the count excludes Freddie
Threepwood's impersonation of his father in 'Lord Emsworth
Acts for the Best'.

38. George Ovens's pub, the Emsworth Arms, was famed for its
home-brewed ale, served at all times of the day and night. It
faced severe competition for business from the eleven other
pubs in Market Blandings or Blandings Parva (Beetle and
Wedge, Blue Boar, Blue Cow, Blue Dragon, Cow and
Grasshopper, Goat and Feathers, Goose and Gander, Jolly
Cricketers, Stitch in Time, Waggoners' Rest and Wheatsheaf),
but as Wodehouse wrote:

> In most English country towns, if the public-houses do not
> actually out-number the inhabitants, they all do an
> excellent trade. It is only when they are two to one that hard
> times hit them and set the innkeepers blaming the
> Government.

39. This demonstrates that Wodehouse was fully aware of the
full scale of the misery he had brought down on the heads of
Clarence and Galahad by introducing their ninth and tenth
sisters into the book, even though the tenth was the pleasant
Diana. Readers familiar with the canon will undoubtedly have
their own views as to the identity of the four described as being
'as bad as Brenda'.

40. Some things will never change.

41. Wodehouse had a classical education and would no doubt
have remembered in time that the Gorgon in Greek mythology
turned people to stone, not ice. This would have necessitated
further amendments in a few paragraphs in this chapter and
again, for example, in chapter 9.

42. This sentence is a good example of Wodehouse 'writing
short'. In later drafts he would have made much more of this
action sequence. In a number of instances both before and after
the Second World War, Wodehouse was either commissioned to
write a novelette of some 25,000 to 30,000 words (such as
Laughing Gas), or to condense a full-length novel of 70,000

words for pre-publication as a magazine one-shotter (e.g., *Cocktail Time* or *Ring for Jeeves*). The sixteen chapters of *Sunset at Blandings*, at the stage to which Wodehouse had brought them when he went into hospital, are reminiscent of the one-shotters in pace and discipline. He would have had every intention of filling out the chapters and slowing down the book.

43. The typescript here is scored out, and the handwritten correction indecipherable. But a page of the notes provides an alternative: 'the older Mr Bessemer's companies'.

44. Three times in these chapters Wodehouse equates a character's look of despondency with the Mona Lisa, and he has done the same in several earlier novels. In *The Code of the Woosters* it is clear that Bertie has learned this piece of imagery from Jeeves, but Jeeves, Bertie and Wodehouse have all got it wrong. Walter Pater's *Studies in the History of the Renaissance* had been published in 1873, and no doubt the passage about the sensuous Mona Lisa was already being set for boys to render into scholarly Greek by the time Wodehouse had reached the Dulwich sixth-form. Richard Usborne's guess is that Wodehouse misremembered a passage, substituting 'Hers is the head upon which all the *sorrows* of the world are come' for the true '. . . all the *ends of the world* are come'.

Usborne goes on to comment how odd it was that the error should have superseded the production of the Cole Porter/Wodehouse/Guy Bolton musical comedy *Anything Goes*, which the couplet in its song *You're the Top*.

> You're the Nile, you're the Tower of Pisa,
> You're the smile on the Mona Lisa . . .

45. No mention has previously been made of a croquet lawn at Blandings. Clock golf, bowling and tennis court only.

46. There are not too many ghosts in Wodehouse. Perhaps the most useful, if least well documented, was Lady Agatha, the wife of Sir Caradoc the Crusader, whose supposed appearances in the ruined chapel at Rowcester Abbey were instrumental in the building's sale to the American rotationist Mrs Spottsworth.

47. The songwriter was Noel Coward, the song 'Mad Dogs and Englishmen'. The rhyme was one that Wodehouse, himself a

past master lyric-writer ('lyrist' was the term he used), very much admired:

> In tropical climes there are certain times of day
> When all the citizens retire
> To tear their clothes off and perspire
> It's one of those rules that the greatest fools obey,
> Because the sun is much too sultry
> And one must avoid its ultry-violet ray.

48. Why can't he call Jeff 'Jeff'? He might be Jeff Smith. It's the surname, Bennison, which might remind Lord Emsworth of the man, Jeff's father, who got away with thousands of pounds of his cash.

49. Wrykyn was the college which Wodehouse based on Dulwich, and was the setting for three novels and twelve short stories. A number of its old boys appeared in 'adult' novels, such as Sam Shotter in *Sam the Sudden*.

50. It is not clear why Gally should say that Jeff was after a job as Lord Emsworth's secretary. Why not say 'to paint the Empress'?

Lord Emsworth's secretaries are a transient lot, rarely staying in their posts for more than one book. The list includes Rupert Baxter, Psmith, Hugo Carmody, Monty Bodkin, Jerry Vail, Lavender Briggs and Sandy Callender.

51. This is the first Bentley reported as belonging to the Castle. Appearances have previously been made by an Antelope and a Hispano-Suiza (both in *Summer Lightning*). But more to the point, perhaps, is to ask the question: if Gally could borrow the Bentley to go to London, why could he not have borrowed it to go to Eastbourne, a more difficult journey by rail whether it was on the east or south coast. We know the answer – it is so that Gally could meet Claude Duff and discover that Claude knew Jeff Bennison. On reflection, Wodehouse would surely have chosen a more subtle way of introducing this plant.

52. It must be assumed that Wodehouse would also have set up a plausible explanation for Jeff Bennison's apparent awareness of J. B. Underwood's reputation as a womanizer.

53. See 'Pig-Hoo-o-o-o-ey', *Heavy Weather* and *Pigs Have Wings*.

54. Gally's reference to Freddie as Vicky's cousin extends the

courtesy family relationships mentioned in note 17, for remember there was no blood connection between the Threepwoods and Vicky Underwood.

55. The Bill Lister incident in *Full Moon*.

56. An example of the confusion which results in writing about too many sisters. Prudence Garland's mother was Dora, but she was not present when this incident occurred. It was to Veronica Wedge's mother Hermione that Freddie spilt the beans.

57. Rooks' eggs are green mottled with olive. Bill-stamps were a violet indigo-blue colour from ink-pads for rubber stamping the backs of cheques, a sight which few of us see today.

58. In his typescript Wodehouse had a big cross against the next four lines of dialogue, and the word 'fix' scrawled in large letters. It is not clear what difficulty he had identified here, for 'fix' meant 'Do it again and get it right'.

59. Blissful Blandings weather: hammocks by day and a warm moon at night! The Californian climate is normal for Wodehouse's England, especially in Shropshire. Changes in the weather are always purposeful, as on page 77 to get Jeff off the terrace and to the realization that he has been locked out. On page 47 the strong sunshine is used to facilitate Sir James Piper's entrance.

In *Summer Lightning* a sudden downpour of rain drives the sundered lovers into each other's arms in a deserted cottage in the West Wood. In *Full Moon*, if you can believe Prudence Garland, a fortnight of persistent rain had driven Freddie Threepwood to propose marriage to his first cousin Veronica Wedge 'as a way of passing the time when bored with backgammon'.

60. A number of minor points would have required attention before the final draft. In three previous appearances (*Pigs Have Wings*, *Galahad at Blandings* and *A Pelican at Blandings*) the originator of the diet has been spelt 'Wolff-Lehmann'. The original report had proposed a daily 57,800 calories, but this was later reduced to 5,700 in *Galahad*, and increased again, though only to 57,000, in *Pelican*. Interestingly, while the first three reports agree on the need for 4lb 5oz of proteins to be included along with 25lb of carbohydrates, the draft in this book suggests proteins of 4lb 7oz. Surely the editors would have reverted to at least 57,000 calories and 4lb 5oz.

61. The fifty-one-year-old Seventh Baronet of Much Matchingham has been considered by some, including Richard Usborne, to be the nobleman who has been subjected to more unwarranted suspicion and downright denigration than any other in the whole peerage. Such has been the success of the strong campaign against him, they argue, that even the publishing house of Herbert Jenkins Ltd stated, in a synopsis at the beginnings of *Pigs Have Wings*, that 'on previous occasions the unscrupulous baronet has made determined efforts to nobble Lord Emsworth's pig'. But when one comes to review the facts, whatever the truth of this particular charge, the life of the Bart has hardly been a picture of injured innocence.

The accusation concerning his alleged doctoring of Galahad Threepwood's dog Towser may remain unproven, but it is high up on the list of the distinctly probable, and his reaction to the threat of the publication of Gally's memoirs (in which he is featured in five separate chapters: 4, 7, 11, 18 and 24) is enough to convince us that the other charges against him in his youth would stick. Consider in addition the following list of matters which cast serious doubts on his adult moral turpitude:

1. The way in which he inveigled George Cyril Wellbeloved into his employment.
2. The way that, while a JP, he nevertheless approved of the theft of the Empress of Blandings.
3. The way in which he provided George Cyril with a shotgun, and instructed him to let intruders have it with both barrels.
4. The way in which he conspired with Lady Constance Keeble and offered Percy Pilbeam £500 to steal Galahad's manuscript.
5. The fact that he had to employ Pilbeam to recover some indiscreet letters to a lady.

With these charges to face, it is difficult to accept the judgement that he was a lively and rather likeable chap, a 'practically blameless bart – one of those who start their lives well, skid for a while and then slide back on to the straight and narrow path and stay there'.

This man evidently lived one jump ahead of the

gendarmerie and sliced bread with a corkscrew. He was variously described as being as slippery as a greased eel, the world's worst twister, a horn-swoggling highbinder, and a sheep-faced, shambling exile from hell who would dope his own grandmother's bran mash and acorns. He never denied that he walked round Romano's with a soup tureen on his head and a stick of celery on his shoulder, claiming to be a Buckingham Palace sentry; or that he purloined Lord Burper's false teeth; or that he was thrown out of the Café de l'Europe for trying to raise the price of a bottle of champagne by raffling his trousers; or did what Galahad remembered, and Beach discovered, in what is known as the story of the prawns. We are not certain which of these incidents were perpetrated during his membership of the Pelican Club, but there can be little doubt that he approached the question of living from a starting point considerably in advance even of most of the other members of that liberal society.

This 6'1" snake got fatter day by day in every way, pausing only briefly to consider the suggestion by his fiancée, Gloria Salt, that she would scratch the fixture if he continued to look like a captive balloon, and ignoring completely the comment that a girl marrying him would be in danger of being charged with bigamy. He was never fond of Galahad (not only regarding him as a — and as an ———, but a ****** and an !!!!!! as well) or Clarence, which was all right by them.

To set against all this, on the credit side, he could fairly claim to have won the fat pumpkin prize at the Shrewsbury Agricultural Show three times in a row, to have looked askance at Lord Emsworth's beard and, a fact over which he had no control, to be the uncle of the truly misunderstood Monica Simmons and Monty Bodkin. His belated marriage to Maudie Stubbs can be regarded as neutral at best, for there is evidence that he had gambled a portion of the honeymoon money put aside for their celebrations on a horse; and it may well have been the after-effects of his private celebration on winning £100 which caused the '4' he claimed to have written in his letter to Maudie specifying the date of their marriage to have been read by her naked eye as '7', thereby causing the wedding to be postponed for some decades. Furthermore, he admitted that it was only because Maudie seemed to *understand* ambrosia chiffon pie that he realized they were twin souls and that he should finally be man enough to repair the damage of the past.

62. A flask of strong drink emptied into the Empress's food trough, in *Galahad at Blandings*.

63. Lord Emsworth's favourite book has been referred to in the texts variously as Whiffle's *On the Care of the Pig*, Whiffle's *The Care of the Pig*, *Whiffle on the Care of the Pig* and just *Whiffle*. It is published by Popgood and Grooly, and the true name of its author may remain one of the minor mysteries of English letters.

In *Galahad at Blandings*, not only was the man's name given as Augustus ('Gus' to his friends) Whipple, but it turned out that Galahad knew him. Despite this, he had the nerve to introduce the relevant young hero Sam Bagshott into the Castle as an impostor under the same name. When the real Whipple turned up, anxious to see the splendid prize-winning Empress, of whom he had heard so much, Gally persuaded his brother to write a cheque for £1,000 to supposedly cover Whipple's gambling debts.

In *Sunset at Blandings* we have, literally, Wodehouse's last word on the subject. The author's name appears twice in Wodehouse's own typescript. The first time he is Whiffle. The second time the name is typed as Whipple, but in Wodehouse's characteristic hand the 'pp' has been changed firmly to 'ff'.

64. Wodehouse's irreverent fondness for the law (policemen, magistrates, Justices of the Peace and occasional young barristers) is a constant and varied joy. He gave his JPs extraordinary powers of arrest, sentence and imprisonment, and they were not slow to use, or threaten to use, them. In *Pigs Have Wings* Sir Gregory Parsloe-Parsloe, JP, threatened Beach, Galahad and Lord Emsworth (himself a JP and presumably sitting on the same bench as Sir Gregory) with imprisonment for pig-stealing.

65. Even between old friends it is surely unlikely that Jeff would have been so informal in his reference to one of whom he was in such awe.

66. Sally Fairmile was another who was compared to a Tanagra statuette in *Quick Service*.

67. Bottleton East was where Freddie Widgeon sang at an amateur prize night, accompanied by Jos Waterbury, in 'The

Masked Troubadour'. With his specialist knowledge of the
place he was later able to speak eloquently on the subject to
Leila Yorke in *Ice in the Bedroom*, and discourage her from
taking a bed-sitting-room in its environs to study the martyred
proletariat and soak in squalor through every pore. In addition,
Lord Blicester spoke at election rallies there in the
Conservative interest.

68. Richard Usborne sought to identify this song. Guy Bolton
told him that he could remember it, but not its title, writer,
singer or show. Mr H. G. Bowen was the Chief Cashier of the
Bank of England from 1893 to 1902, and would have had his
signature on all their banknotes during that period. None of the
Guards regiments were able to find any record of it in their
archives. The Adjutant of the First or Grenadier Regiment of
Guards surmised that the writer was not a Guardsman, since
the Guards wear bearskins, not busbies.

   The Research Department of the Music Library at the
British Library, the Performing Rights Society and the BBC
Music Library were all defeated. George Wood, OBE, aided by
Marion Ross as researcher, claimed that the song had been
written by George Simms (author of *It was Christmas Night at
the Workhouse*) and Jay Hickory Wood (biographer of Dan Leno
Senr. and the writer of many libretti for pantomimes) for Dan
Leno as an interpolated number for the pantomime *Dick
Whittington* at Drury lane in 1898/9. But according to the
records, the pantomime at Drury Lane that winter was *The
Forty Thieves*.

69. See *Leave it to Psmith*.

70. See *Galahad at Blandings*.

The Family of the Eighth Earl of Emsworth

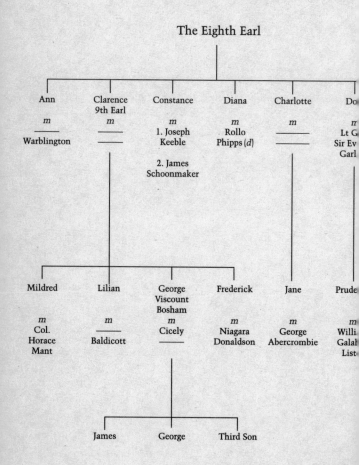

The Eighth Earl

Ann	Clarence 9th Earl	Constance	Diana	Charlotte	Do
m	m	m	m	m	m
Warblington		1. Joseph Keeble	Rollo Phipps (d)		Lt G Sir Ev Garl
		2. James Schoonmaker			

Mildred	Lilian	George Viscount Bosham	Frederick	Jane	Prude
m	m	m	m	m	m
Col. Horace Mant	Baldicott	Cicely	Niagara Donaldson	George Abercrombie	Willi Galah List

James George Third Son

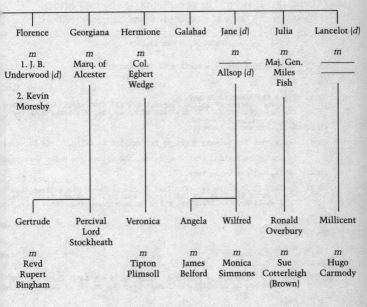

Florence	Georgiana	Hermione	Galahad	Jane (d)	Julia	Lancelot (d)
m	*m*	*m*		*m*	*m*	*m*
1. J. B. Underwood (d)	Marq. of Alcester	Col. Egbert Wedge		——— Allsop (d)	Maj. Gen. Miles Fish	——— ———
2. Kevin Moresby						

Gertrude	Percival Lord Stockheath	Veronica	Angela	Wilfred	Ronald Overbury	Millicent
m		*m*	*m*	*m*	*m*	*m*
Revd Rupert Bingham		Tipton Plimsoll	James Belford	Monica Simmons	Sue Cotterleigh (Brown)	Hugo Carmody

Scenario

Among the papers found in the hospital where P. G. Wodehouse died in 1975 was a group entitled 'Scenario. January 19, 1975'. His comments on the first fifteen chapters, by then at first draft stage, were as follows:

SCENARIO.   Jan 19.1975

Ch 1.   Aziz, with possibly a mention of the bracelet.

Ch 2.   Aziz.

Ch 3.   Gally and Vicky unchanged.
In scene between Gally and Florence out all that about Jeff's father F's objection to Jeff is his lack of money. Out F's husband *handwritten notes*

Ch 4.   Aziz, but can be improved.

Ch 5.   Aziz, but Jeff's name ought to be familiar to Gally. This is where

it should be planted that J's father, the actor, and Gally were pals

Ch6.   Aziz, but can be improved.

Ch 7.   On Page 33 Beach tells Gally Jeff is his nephew. His brother took the name of Bennison for the stage. Beach is agitated, Gally calm. I shall have to think about the uncle-nephew situation.

Ch 8.   Aziz,

Ch 9.   Aziz.

Ch 10. Aziz.

Ch 11. Aziz.

Ch 12. Page 67. If Beach is scared of being found out to be Jeff's uncle, he would not be laughing. Jeff must hear the rumble of Gally's voice.

Ch 12. Aziz.

Ch 14. Aziz up to end of Page 82.

Ch 15. Aziz to end of Page 84, where Florence must be left suspecting Gally but realising that she has no proof.

ALL THE ABOVE SEEMS STRAIGHT

Ch 16. Brenda arrives. Florence tells her about suspecting Jeff but having no proof. Brenda advises her to apply to Dame Daphne. She does so and gets identification. She then goes to Gally and we play the scene 86 to 88.

SCENARIO. Jan 19. 1975

Ch 1. Aziz, with possibly a mention of the bracelet.

Ch 2. Aziz.

Ch 3. Gally and Vicky unchanged.
  In scene between Gally and Florence cut all that about Jeff's father.
  F's objection to Jeff is his lack of money. F's husband is planted [. . . ? . . .]. She tells G he is weak.

Ch 4. Aziz, but can be improved.

Ch 5. Aziz, but Jeff's name ought to be familiar to Gally. This is where it should be planted that J's father, the actor, and Gally were pals.

Ch 6. Aziz, but can be improved.

Ch 7. On Page 33 Beach tells Gally Jeff is his nephew. His brother took the name of Bennison for the stage. Beach is agitated, Gally calm.
  I shall have to think about the uncle-nephew situation.

Ch 8. Aziz.

Ch 9. Aziz.

Ch 10. Aziz.

Ch 11. Aziz.

Ch 12. Page 67. If Beach is scared of being found out to be Jeff's uncle, he would not be laughing. Jeff must hear the rumble of Gally's voice.

Ch 13. Aziz.

Ch 14. Aziz up to end of Page 82.

Ch 15. Aziz to end of Page 84, where Florence must be left suspecting Gally but realizing that she has no proof.

ALL THE ABOVE SEEMS STRAIGHT

Ch 16. Brenda arrives. Florence tells her about suspecting Jeff but having no proof. Brenda advises her to apply to Dame Daphne. She does so and gets identification. She then goes to Gally and we play the scene p 86 to 88.

Scenario (continued)

Ch 17. I haven't quite decided on the order in which events come, but I will
put down a tentative sequence. I think that after leaving Gally
Florence go to Brenda and tell her what has happened. Brenda is
distrait. She says about theft of her necklace, from jewel case left
in hall. • *You can't let this man leave house. He's got my necklace*

Ch 18. Vicky tells Gally she stole necklace to prevent Jeff leaving house
Have them consulting Beach as ot whether this is only for murder.
Gally says he will put necklace in Lord E's study.

*b C. on with Beach as to whom ought is the strain did a things.
on bit of wisdom.*

Ch19. Continue the scene between Brenda and Florence. Florence says
Jeff must have stolen necklace. They decide that Jeff's room must
be searched. By whom? Brenda suggests Claude. Claude sent for. Q

Ch 20. Gally goes to Ld E. Tells him that Florence has fired Jeff. Ld E
furious. Ld E says he will go and see Jeff and assure him that
he won't have to leave. Where is Jeff? he is probably in his room.
'When you have a job like painting the Empress, you have to do a
lot of deep thinking.' They go to Jeff's room. As they reach it,
they hear a crash from inside. Ld E thinks Jeff may have met with
an accident. They go in and find Claude. Gally is stern with Cla
He makes him confess why he is there. He says Brenda told him to
search the room for stolen necklace. L E furious at this slur on
Jeff, rushes off to tackle Brenda. Gally is left to talk to Claude
Tells him he must expect this sort of thing at Blandings.
Use the stuff about meek men?
Ld E returns, says he has properly ticked Brenda off. And now, h
says, to tick Florence off for firing Jeff. Claude left , stunn

Ch 17. I haven't quite decided on the order in which events come, but I will put down a tentative sequence. I think that after leaving Gally Florence go to Brenda and tell her what has happened. Brenda is distrait. She says about theft of her necklace, from jewel case left in hall. **'You can't let this man leave house. He's got my necklace.'**

Ch 18. Vicky tells Gally she stole necklace to prevent Jeff leaving house. Have them consulting Beach as to whether this is only for murder. Gally says he will put necklace in Lord E's study.

Ch 19. Φ **C consults Beach as to where people in tec stories hide things.** *On top of [? wardrobe?*

Continue the scene between Brenda and Florence. Florence says Jeff must have stolen necklace. They decide that Jeff's room must be searched. By whom? Brenda suggests Claude. Claude sent for. Φ

Ch 20. Gally goes to Ld E. Tells him that Florence has fired Jeff. Ld E furious. Ld E says he will go and see Jeff and assure him that he won't have to leave. Where is Jeff? he is probably in his room. 'When you have a job like painting the Empress, you have to do a lot of deep thinking.' They go to Jeff's room. As they reach it, they hear a crash from inside. Ld E thinks Jeff may have met with an accident. They go in and find Claude. Gally is stern with Claude. He makes him confess why he is there. He says Brenda told him to search the room for stolen necklace. Ld E furious at this slur on Jeff, rushes off to tackle Brenda. Gally is left to talk to Claude. Tells him he must expect this sort of thing at Blandings. Use the stuff about meek men?

Ld E returns, says he has properly ticked Brenda off. And, now, he says, to tick Florence off for firing Jeff. Claude left, stunned.

Ch 21.

They go to F's suite, Gally with Ld E to render moral support. Brenda is there. (No, I don't think she need be). F. says Ld E has grossly insulted Brenda. (Yes, I think the scene wd play better without Brenda). F. says Unless Ld E apologizes, Brenda will leave, and if B leaves she, F) will leave. Ld E refuses to apologize and F says she will leave tomorrow morning. ~~They go out together and Gally praises Ld E.~~ The meek men stuff might fi They go out together, G praising Ld E. The meek men stuff might fit in better here.

Ch 22.

G₄ally goes to his hammock. P⁺us Piper, who says he was just goin to propose when Murchison came up with rain coat, saying the sky looked threatening. G says Beach has told him that Murch loves ma and he will keep him away while Piper proposes.

G goes off to tackle Murch. Succeeds. G₄es back to hammock. P₄us Piper says he is engaged. G gets him to give Jeff job of painting his portrait, - and you knos hundreds of rich people, you can recommend Jeff to them. P. agrees. ⌀ ⌀ + Ld E with necklace — Inē.

G sees car draw up at door. Florence comes out and stands wai -ing for Brenda. G. goes to her, tells her that Piper has given Jeff portrair job for princely sum, all his pals in Cabinet will have their portraits painted by Jeff for princely summ, Ld E will pay him highly for Empress and Beach will add his bit as a wedding present. ?Bech is J's uncle.? F gtes into car without a word.

End with G₄lly chatting with Beach.

THE END

122

Ch 21. They go to F's suite, Gally with Ld E to render moral support. Brenda is there. (No, I don't think she need be). F says Ld E has grossly insulted Brenda. (Yes, I think the scene wd play better without Brenda). F says Unless Ld E apologizes, Brenda will leave, and if B leaves she, F, will leave. Ld E refuses to apologize and F says she will leave tomorrow morning.

+ *X from cupboard. He ticks Ld E off for wanting pig in gallery)*

    The meek men stuff might fit. They go out together, G praising Ld E. The meek men stuff might fit in better here.

Ch 22. Gally goes to his hammock. Plus Piper, who says he was just going to propose when Murchison came up with rain coat, saying the sky looked threatening. G says Beach has told him that Murch loves maid, and he will keep him away while Piper proposes.

    G goes off to tackle Murch. Succeeds. Goes back to hammock. Plus Piper says he is engaged. G gets him to give Jeff job of painting his portrait, – and you know hundreds of rich people, you can recommend Jeff to them. P agrees. Φ Φ + *Ld E with necklace. – Ld E.*

    G sees car draw up at door. Florence comes out and stands waiting for Brenda. G. goes to her, tells her that Piper has given Jeff portrait job for princely sum, all his pals in Cabinet will have their portraits painted by Jeff for princely sum, Ld E will pay him highly for Empress and Beach will add his bit as a wedding present. ? Beach is J's uncle. ? F gets into car without a word.

    End with Gally chatting with Beach.

THE END

Further Relevant Working Notes

From the comments in Chapter 3 and the note
concerning Chapter 21 it is clear that the author has not
yet worked out just how Kevin Moresby, Florence
Moresby's second husband, should fit into the story. The
following two facsimile manuscript notes show two
completely different approaches that he had
contemplated at different times.

Husband

Clipped moustache. V. military. Appearance
misleading, as he was a v. wild man. Very gib and
strong.

Vegetarian. F. disapproved. Ridiculous fad! (He has
become a vegn).

Gally says I was a vegn for a while many years ago
because I cd not afford not to be, meat costing so
much. (My investments on the turf

Kevin: Dt you think there is any hope of a
    reconciliation?
Gally: It depends what the row was about. If you have
    been preferring blondes.
K: Good heavens, no.
G: Then what was the trouble?
K: I became converted to vegetarianism and F
    called it a ridiculous fad.
G: *You didn't* try to convert *her* to veg.
K: Certainly not.
G tells K to hide in F's suite and jump out at her.
    Drink G. Ovens beer.

Florence's husband.

He is Florence's nephew, an author, or playwright? (need he be B's nephew?)
Gally meets him in Club. He has chucked his, & supper, or invited on a
Strewn of moment, — he has gone to B's party to creadditi in pott. (Gally does
not know his father). (Wanted to flaviir, chivalry out)

Problem. Why have — call his 'husband' + a split? And how does
this reconciliation suggest Jagg?

∮ It looks as if they are only married, E.V. Shall he have already abconded &
by getting him to polu of money to save him if we even or perm he plu, it plagmin—

His appearances ∮ (1) In club. (2) At Dunstable arms after Piper
has left V & is alone. (3) In big scenes (she 2 F. has advised him to
throw up Gabriel boat)

∮ They are only engaged. Can they have split + she tell him to go and
make he B give up idea & stay in present Gally? In big scene he reveals
true to her, out he agrees to pull a strong ∮

∮ I can cure Gloz anxiety with him re conviction to & B, — which
will make P. melt to him.

X In Emco Arms Scene 'husband' has S. all out his friend with P.
In G. F meet, says he was weak.

∮ and X are Emco Arms. ∮ advises X to shake up in ∮t pott — Rida

Florence's husband

He is Beach's nephew, an actor, or playwright? (need he be B's nephew?)

Gally meets him in Ch. 2. F. has chucked him, if engaged or insisted on a divorce if married, & he has gone to B's pantry for consolation & port. (Gally does not know his father). (Husband is leaving, chucked out)

Problem, why have – call him 'husband' – & F split?
Φ And how does their reconciliation affect Jeff?
Φ It looks as if they aren't married. Qy. Shall he have already alienated F? by getting her to put up money to star him if an actor or finance his play, if playwright.

His appearance (1) in Ch 2 (2) At Emsworth Arms after Piper has left & G is alone. (2) In big scene. (In 2 G. has advised him to stoke up on G. Ovens beer)

Φ They are only engaged. Can they have split ∵ she told him to go and make Ld E give up idea of pig in portrait gallery? In big scene he reveals that he has got Ld E to agree to have the pig in study. Φ

Φ I can see good comedy with him reasoning with Ld E, – which wd make F. melt to him.

X in Ems Arms scene 'husband' tells G all abt his quarrel with F.
In G-F F merely says he was weak.

G and X at Ems Arms. G advises X to stoke up on G's port & hide.

He then proposes to have Kevin (referred to as 'X')
play a part in the 'Big Scene' as follows:

    Big Scene.
    Start with Ld E and G entering.
    Row. Don't have F saying she will leave. Work up
to where F. says something abt pig being in portrait
gallery.
    X comes out of cupboard.
    'I wd like to say a few words on that subject.'
    X reasons with Lord E.
    Ld E convinced. Goes off to break it to Jeff that his
portrait won't be in gallery. He will be disappointed
    X and F reconciled.
    X says Let's get married and go to USA. Put on my
play there.
    F says you won't mind V being with us. Can't
leave her here with Jeff.
    X and F go off, leaving Gally.
    Gally muses. Plug snag of Jeff and V being parted.

How Richard Usborne saw the Evolution of the Plot

When *Sunset at Blandings* was first published, Richard Usborne explained the processes through which the draft still had to go before it would have been regarded by Wodehouse as a satisfactorily complete novel. He first analysed the stage which had been reached, and the snags which remained, at the time of the 19 January Scenario (pages 118 to 123). At that time, he wrote, Wodehouse:

1. is proposing to give his hero, Jeff, a less reprobate father. The father will now be Beach the butler's brother, and an actor rather than an absconding company director. But it is not clear from the scenario why Beach is 'agitated' about this. Is it because he thinks that Lady Florence will oppose the Jeff/Vicky romance even more strongly if she discovers that Jeff, in addition to being penniless and an impostor, is also nephew to the castle's butler?

2. has not decided what to do about Florence's husband. After some doubts he is clearly going to *be* her husband, and somehow their separation has to be changed to reconciliation and bright hopes of happiness together in the future;

3. has left Claude Duff in the air and unattached;

4. has not decided how Jeff is going to assure himself of an income sufficient to enable him honourably to marry the soon-to-be-rich Vicky. If other objections (see 1 above) are overcome, Florence

might believe Gally's enthusiastic assurances about Jeff's future in Chapter 22, at least for long enough to loosen the purse-strings as trustee of Vicky's inheritance. But Jeff, by the Wodehouse code, can't marry and be an heiress's kept man;

5. has not allowed for an 'all-our-troubles-are-over' love scene for Jeff and Vicky;

6. has not yet 'planted' Brenda's bracelet (or necklace), the stealing of which is to bring down the curtain on Act 2, so to speak, and provided good alarums and excursions at the beginning of the final Act;

7. has scarcely touched on the necessary romance of Sergeant Murchison and Marilyn Poole. That chauffeur, of whom Murchison is jealous, is a dark horse. Will he be developed?

8. has left Brenda, Piper's sister, at a loose end. It is not like the benign Wodehouse to leave even such an unrewarding character as Brenda unrewarded with an autumn romance of her own. After all, Constance, who has harassed, bullied and dominated Lord Emsworth from book to book, story to story, is allowed to marry two nice American millionaires successively. And the awful Roderick Spode, in the Bertie Wooster books, has his Madeline Bassett to dream about. Brenda, in this book, would surely be smiling when last seen. And her brother's successful courtship of Diana will not be enough to keep that smile on her face for long. James and Diana are *not* likely to want her to come and live with them at Number 11 Downing Street;

9. has not settled whether the Empress's portrait is going to please Lord Emsworth this time and, if so, whether he will hang it triumphantly in the family portrait gallery or have it, less triumphantly, in his study.

He then related this to the normal development of a Blandings novel.

> We are back in a favourite Blandings theme – the heroine brought to the castle to keep her away, and cool her off, from the penniless hero; the infiltration of the castle by the hero in some guise, organized by Galahad (or Lord Ickenham); the weaving of the web of deceit, false names, false purposes, 'telling the tale'; the recognition scene when the impostor is unmasked; the theft of something valuable (Lord Emsworth's pig, Gally's Memoirs, a sister's necklace) which, being found and restored, makes the just rejoice, the unjust look silly and the right couples able to marry happily.

> How to get the heroine's loved one into the castle without the fierce hostess knowing that he is the man the heroine is here to forget is the recurrent problem in Blandings novels. It is no good letting Lord Emsworth into the conspiracy. He would sooner or later give it away, by mistake, to his sister.

> So he has to be fooled too. In this novel, Wodehouse is toying with, even muddling, two ideas which he has used before: the infiltration of the castle by the hero as an artist to paint the Empress, as Bill Lister in *Full Moon*, or as a candidate for the job of Lord Emsworth's secretary, as Jerry Vail in *Pigs Have Wings*.

> For some reason Gally tells Claude Duff that Jeff is at the castle trying for the secretary job when Jeff is already installed as the artist to paint the Empress.

Usborne then used the Scenario and other notes to suggest how the remaining chapters might have evolved. Briefly, this summary proceeds as follows:

As the last sentence of Chapter 16 shows, Vicky has some minutes' start on Gally and must act without his advice. Gally has only just learnt that Florence has rumbled Jeff's alias. Vicky has had time to remove a necklace from the jewel case that Brenda has carelessly left in the hall. Her purpose is to delay, if not prevent, Jeff's being given marching orders by his hostess, her step-mother. No suspect will be allowed to leave the castle until the necklace is found, and Jeff is without doubt going to be suspected.

Vicky tells Gally that she has pinched the necklace, and she gives it to him. He puts it in some obvious place in Lord Emsworth's study. Brenda discovers the loss of the necklace and the finger of suspicion points to Jeff, by now known to be Vicky's demon lover, in need of money, and at the Castle under an assumed name. Florence and Brenda decide to ask Claude Duff to search Jeff's room for the necklace. Jeff is still not aware that Brenda and Florence know that he is an impostor, let alone that they have told Vicky that he is to be kicked out of the castle immediately. He does not know anything about any necklace, nor that Vicky has stolen it to make it inconvenient for him to be allowed to leave.

Gally tells Lord Emsworth that Florence has told the man who is, at last, painting his beloved pig's portrait, and is anyway his, Lord Emsworth's, guest, to leave. This is where Lord Emsworth begins to see red and become the dominant male. He slates Brenda for having put Claude on to search a guest's room. Brenda goes and complains to Florence, and while she slates him for having been rude to Brenda, he slates her for attempting to kick Jeff out.

Inspired by Ovens's home-brew beer and urged on by Galahad, Florence's husband Kevin has sneaked into the castle to plead with his estranged wife, and has hidden himself in a cupboard in her room. He hears Lord Emsworth slating her, and he emerges in his wrath from the cupboard and, pending his appeal to Florence, he wades into Lord Emsworth for his harsh words to her. When Florence gets over her shock at seeing her husband coming out of a cupboard, she stands amazed by the man's courage in giving Lord Emsworth the rough of his tongue.

Lord Emsworth leaves Florence's room, shaking his head. But he returns in a moment to say, 'Is this the necklace you're all making such a lot of trouble about? I found it in my study. Very careless to leave it about, whoever did.'

Florence and Brenda leave the castle with Kevin in a fury against Lord Emsworth, Gally and Jeff. We assume that Kevin will henceforth dominate railway porters, head-waiters and the actors in, and the producers of, his instantly successful plays. He will also dominate the willing Florence, his ever-to-be-loving wife. But his first act of dominance over her has been to persuade her to give her blessing to Vicky and Jeff's marriage and to release Vicky's money to her. It was Gally who helped Kevin to win back his wife and Kevin owes it to Gally to fix that for him. Lord Emsworth, despite being bawled out by Kevin, will have forgotten everybody and everything within a few days of being left in peace, perfect peace, alone or with just Gally in his own castle.

It would create a bit of a problem in Wodehouse's strict code of morals if Vicky and Jeff were left together at the end of this book, chaperoned only by males (Lord Emsworth, Gally and Beach).

Usborne believes that Wodehouse would have developed Claude Duff's role, and built him up in a number of scenes throughout the book. He guesses that:

In an early chapter Vicky had begged to be allowed to ask a school friend to come and stay with her in her captivity, which her step-mother was only too glad to grant. On arrival she is welcomed by all as providing a modicum of chaperonage for Vicky when Diana goes back with Sir James, taking Murchison and Marilyn Poole with them. Claude might be expected to have accompanied them, too, but there is just time, before they leave, for him to lose his heart as suddenly to Vicky's friend as he did to Vicky. So he doesn't go back with his boss. Sir James, in a yeasty benevolence as a result of his own approaching nuptials, gives Claude prolonged leave.

So Jeff stays on and finishes the Empress's portrait, with Vicky in the background during working hours. Claude and Vicky's friend stay on the premises too. And then, in addition to the portraits that Jeff is asked to paint, of Sir James Piper for a start and then, Gally hopes, of all the other members of the Cabinet, Claude gets Jeff the job of Advertising Manager of Duff & Trotter, where the money is good and steady and he can pay his whack with Vicky as man and wife.

Usborne finally sought to tidy up a few loose ends which relate to the regular characters who appeared in the Blandings series. In particular, the Empress's portrait will now:

hang in the family portrait gallery. Lord Emsworth can enjoy looking at it whenever he is not out at the sty looking at its sitter. Gally and Beach ring down the curtain over a glass or two of port in the pantry. Beach might now be distantly step-related to Gally (and Lord Emsworth, Florence, Connie and all the other eight sisters), but he will continue to be the supreme butler. McAllister is still (we assume, for we have not heard of him for a while) head gardener, though his cousin Niagara Donaldson had married Freddie Threepwood who spends most of his time in America, to the great satisfaction of his father. And Beach's niece, Maudie Stubbs (Maudie Montrose of the Criterion bar) is, we believe, Lady Parsloe-Parsloe at Matchingham Hall, just across the fields from the castle.

The notes on Pages 99 to 135 were originally compiled by Richard Usborne and have been revised and updated by Tony Ring.

Blandings

Blandings Castle has joined 221B Baker Street, Dotheboys Hall and Brideshead as one of the landmarks of English literature. Every Wodehouse enthusiast knows its flag-tower, amber drawing-room, terraces, lake and gracious lawns. While I would not dream of joining in the heated debate over Baker Street, the origins of Dotheboys Hall and Brideshead have been firmly traced to places that Dickens and Waugh knew.

Wodehouse, like most authors, drew on his own experience to provide a background for his stories. He left school and wrote school stories; joined a bank and wrote *Psmith in the City*. He went to New York and produced stories about a young writer in New York. He moved to Cannes and we read of Bingo Little and Freddie Widgeon losing their shirt at the tables.

In a letter to his friend Bill Townend, he said he liked using real houses in his novels. It saved time and avoided mistakes. It meant he did not have a character coming in a door at one side of the room in chapter four and leaving by another door in chapter sixteen.

By tracing his movements from letters and biographies, by walking where he had walked, we can identify nearly every setting in his ninety-eight books. He used his own house in Norfolk Street for Lord Emsworth's London address, he installed Aunt Dahlia in the London house of his friend Ian Hay. Bertie Wooster's flat in Berkeley Street is at number 15 where Wodehouse stayed in 1922, while the sphinxes still guard the door of Peacehaven in Mulberry Grove (the second house on the right in Acacia Road, Dulwich).

An original for Blandings somewhere began to look increasingly probable, a theory confirmed when Wodehouse, towards the end of his life, said that Blandings was 'a mixture of places I remembered'. From then on it was a matter not of 'if', but simply 'where'.

The honour of being the original of Blandings has been claimed for many stately homes. Any identification, therefore, must not just present a good case, but also demonstrate that the castle and grounds couldn't be anywhere else.

Blandings first appeared in *Something Fresh* in 1915, but a castle remarkably like it, Dreever Castle, featured in *A Gentleman Of Leisure* five years earlier. This was the first factor in my search – that Blandings had to be somewhere Wodehouse had known before 1910.

Unfortunately, Wodehouse did not have a settled childhood. His father was a magistrate in Hong Kong and, in common with the children of most colonial civil servants, Wodehouse was sent back to England to be brought up by relatives. It may seem heartless to us today, but before the advent of air conditioning very few European children survived in the tropics.

Between 1883 and 1900 he lived, stayed with relatives or was at school at: Bath; Croydon; The Channel Islands; Kearsney, near Dover; Cheney Court, near Box, Wiltshire; Hanley Castle, Worcestershire; Bratton Fleming in Devon; Dulwich; and Stableford in Shropshire. Between leaving school in 1900 and 1910 (*A Gentleman Of Leisure*), he stayed or lived at: Cheltenham; Emsworth, Hampshire; London; and New York; with various visits to the Cotswolds; Jersey; and Lyme Regis.

That long list meant that Blandings, or the sources of Blandings, could be anywhere south of a line drawn from London to Shrewsbury. Another complication was his statement that he set Blandings in Shropshire: 'because I was so happy there as a boy'.

So Blandings is to be found elsewhere. But how much is elsewhere? The castle? Its interior? The library, or the amber drawing-room? The estate and grounds? The local newspaper that records the triumphs of the Empress of Blandings is the *Bridgnorth, Shifnal and Albrighton Argus*. These three Shropshire towns lie around Stableford, where the Wodehouses lived from 1896 to 1902. Did Wodehouse use any other local features to create Blandings? Whatever the answer, it was clear that it would be unwise to concentrate on Shropshire alone.

One factor proved invaluable – Blandings doesn't have a moat. This saved a lot of time. If there had been a moat, Wodehouse would certainly have used it. Moats are good comic material. Heroes and villains can fall into them, heroines can be rescued from them. When Wodehouse did come to know a house with a moat (Hunstanton Hall in Norfolk) he used it at once. Hunstanton also provides a useful clue to the way he hid his sources. It is the setting for three short stories: 'Jeeves and the Old School Chum', 'Mr Potter Takes a Rest Cure' and 'Jeeves and the Impending Doom'. It is clearly recognizable in each, but the house and estate are minor factors in the plot.

Money for Nothing is different. Wodehouse set the novel at Hunstanton with the house and grounds playing an essential part. He must have realized that he had drawn it accurately enough for people to recognize it, so he used the first page of the book to shift the whole establishment over to the Worcestershire–Gloucestershire border.

The only sure method to find the sources of Blandings was to do it the hard way. And the hard way meant spending months of lunchtimes in the British Library slowly grinding through the serried ranks of the Victoria County Histories and other guidebooks for every county south of my London–Shrewsbury line.

By discounting all the houses and castles with moats,

the stately homes and estates that clearly bore no resemblance to Blandings, I eventually reduced the list to thirty. They stretched from Cholmondeley Castle in Cheshire southwards, down both sides of the Severn valley to Berkeley Castle and Sudeley Castle in Gloucestershire. Having eliminated about three hundred candidates that were clearly not Blandings, it was time to go and look at those that were left.

It was at this point that I learned that Wodehouse had said that Blandings owed something to Corsham Court, the home of Lord Methuen, where he had gone skating as a boy. That sent me racing down to Wiltshire to have a closer look.

Corsham Court is a splendid Jacobean building. It has an earl, a rose garden, an enormous yew hedge and a lake. But it is not Blandings. It stands on the edge of the town of Corsham, the grounds bear no resemblance to those at Blandings and it is certainly not a castle. But, if one stands by the lake on a winter evening, the house seems to rear up, filling the horizon as a sombre brooding presence, just as it appeared to unhappy heroes and heroines in the novels. It is a source, but a minor one. I still had to go and look at the others on my list.

The journey of eight hundred miles (there are surprisingly few bridges over the River Severn) gave me the chance to admire, but discard, dozens of beautiful buildings and picturesque estates. There was nothing in Cheshire or north Shropshire, but I had high hopes of the great houses lying to the east of Bridgnorth, near Stableford, where Wodehouse was so happy as a boy. Within a few miles radius lie Aldenham Park, Stanley Hall, Apley Park, Davenport House, Quatford Castle, Dudmaston, Rudge Hall, Gatacre, Patshull, Chillington and Weston Park. Somewhere among these splendid estates there had to be something.

Apley Park, over the river from Bridgnorth, has been suggested, but it is not a castle (though the Gothic castellations deceive many). It was built three hundred years too late, stands on a steep bank directly above the River Severn and there is nothing in the grounds to remind us of Blandings. I drove on to look at the remaining great houses without success – until I came to Weston Park.

Throughout years of reading Blandings stories, certain scraps of description had stuck in my mind. I have no idea why. Perhaps they just struck me as unusual. In the first Blandings story, for instance, Ashe Marson and Joan Peters arrive at the castle in an open cart. The cart takes them along the drive and they see lights from the windows, but then: 'Arriving within sight of the Castle, the cart began a detour . . .' which eventually takes them round the castle to the cobble stones at the rear. One expects the drive to lead up to the front door rather than swing away from it. For some reason, this small detail stuck in my mind and it is exactly what happens at Weston Park. Was it Wodehouse's recollection of accompanying his parents to dinner some dark night in the 1890s?

Like Blandings, Weston Park is the home of an earl, the Earl of Bradford. The house is a gracious red-brick building in the classical style. It is not a castle, but Weston Park is certainly one of the places we are looking for. If you want to see the Blandings terraces looking out over a sunlit park, the lake, the boathouse, the Greek temple, the shady lawn with Gally's cedar tree, go to Weston Park. I still remember the shock of recognition as I drove up to the house. It was like visiting a strange country where the first person you meet in the street is your oldest friend. *This* was the setting in which Wodehouse had placed his castle.

But there are a dozen stately homes in the area. How can we be sure that Weston Park is the one he remembered so vividly?

Firstly, the local vicar was related to the Wodehouses.

Secondly, an uncle of Wodehouse's married the Countess of Bradford's oldest friend and the Visitors' Book shows they stayed at Weston Park often. Either reason would have been sufficient to put the family on the Countess of Bradford's guest list – and we know that Wodehouse accompanied his parents to garden parties and social events at the stately homes nearby. These two factors, though significant, are merely corroborative. The proof is that Wodehouse, always accurate in his descriptions, tells us Blandings has:

> a lake with boathouse in sight of the house;
> a Greek temple overlooking the lake;
> a drive that aims towards the house then swings away from it before bending back to pass down the side of the house;
> a pond in the kitchen garden;
> a small hamlet, Blandings Parva, adjoining the house and gardens, but not on the normal approach to the house (this is Weston-under-Lizard);
> terraces with rosebeds in front of the house;
> steps from these terraces down to a lawn shaded by a cedar tree;
> a thick shrubbery separating the lawn from the kitchen gardens;
> rhododendron bushes at the edge of the terraces which shield a car as it drives away;
> a cottage in the adjoining wood, suitable for concealing stolen pigs or diamond necklaces (the Swiss Cottage);
> the Shrewsbury road nearby (the A5 runs alongside the kitchen garden);
> a stable yard near enough the house for a secretary to be shot with an airgun from the butler's pantry;
> a view of the Wrekin in the distance;
> a pigsty or pigsties in the kitchen gardens just behind the house;

a journey time (in the 1920s) of forty-five minutes by
car to Shrewsbury;

a four-hour trip on the main line from Paddington to
Market Blandings via Oxford (Wodehouse travelled
regularly on this line from 1896–1902 when he was at
school in Dulwich and living at Stableford. In 1960, it
was still three and a half hours to Albrighton or
Shifnal, the two nearest towns).

All these factors are to be found at Weston Park – and
only at Weston Park. But I still had a castle to find.

I drove south to Quatford Castle, Arley Castle, Witley
Court, Madresfield (the original of Brideshead), Croome
D'Abitot, Eastnor Castle, Thornbury Castle, Berkeley
Castle, Toddington and then, with hope fading, I came
to my last candidate – Sudeley Castle in
Gloucestershire. And at Sudeley I found my castle.

It was the same shock of recognition that I had had at
Weston Park, yet I remember my first comment as I
drove up to it was: 'It's the wrong way round.' For some
reason I had thought the ruined wing was on the left of
the castle. It isn't, it is on the right, because Sudeley is
Blandings Castle as surely as Weston Park is the
Blandings estate.

Wodehouse spent many of his school holidays with a
clerical uncle at Hanley Castle, only about fourteen
miles away across the valley. Perhaps he came to know
Sudeley then. However, I think it more likely that he
saw it first when his parents moved to Cheltenham in
1902. He was living in London at that time but he
visited them regularly. It was at Cheltenham that he
watched the Warwickshire cricketer Percy Jeeves, whose
surname he was to make immortal.

In *A Gentleman Of Leisure*, Jimmy Pitt and Molly
McEachern meet near Dreever Castle. They walk on to
look down on the castle from the hillside. This puzzled
me for years, since castles are normally built on high

ground for defence. There are very few you can look down on from a neighbouring hillside and Sudeley is one of them.

I believe the answer lies in the fact that Wodehouse, like his father, was a great walker. I have met one lady who remembered him walking ten or twelve miles as a matter of course. If, as I believe, Wodehouse walked over Cleeve Hill from Cheltenham, then this is how he would have seen Sudeley (the current Sudeley brochure has a picture taken from the same spot).

Blandings Castle has to fulfil the following criteria:

'built in the middle of the fifteenth century' (Sudeley was built in 1441);

within walking distance of somewhere Wodehouse lived or stayed;

a castle which you can look down on from the neighbouring hillside (the best view is from the road up the hill to the Belas Knap earthwork);

able to be reached by train from Paddington (it is Paddington via Oxford for Shropshire; Paddington via Swindon for Cheltenham; and that simple fact solves the railway question that has puzzled so many enthusiasts);

it stands at 'the south end of the Vale of Blandings' (there are no vales in Shropshire, but Sudeley stands at the south end of the Vale of Evesham);

it is 'not ten miles' from Winstone Court (the *Gazeteer* has only one Winstone in England, nine miles from Sudeley);

it possesses: a flag tower which looks out over the river valley,

a ruined wing,

a chapel in the grounds,

famous yew walks.

Sudeley Castle – and *only* Sudeley Castle – meets all these requirements.

Once found, Corsham Court, Weston Park and Sudeley Castle were obvious. Each was only a few miles away from where Wodehouse lived in his youth. He knew Corsham from his childhood with his grandmother and four aunts at Cheney Court. When his parents returned from Hong Kong they lived at Stableford, just a few miles from Weston Park, with whom they shared family acquaintances. When they moved to Cheltenham in 1902, they may or may not have known the Dent-Brocklehursts of Sudeley Castle. But their son certainly saw Sudeley from the same spot as his hero Jimmy Pitt saw it in *A Gentleman Of Leisure*. No wonder the recent TV version of *Heavy Weather* was made at Sudeley.

In the 1960s, the BBC did a TV series of Blandings stories with Ralph Richardson playing Lord Emsworth and Stanley Holloway as his pigman. The BBC did their homework very well. They looked for the features of the Blandings estate and used Weston Park because it fitted exactly.

Now we know why.

N. T. P. MURPHY

The Empress of Blandings

I began to suspect there might be an original for the Empress of Blandings when I learned of Wodehouse's anxiety to avoid factual errors in his stories. He took great pains over detail and several letters to friends exist asking them what a character would wear, see or do in a certain setting. He wrote of dogs and cats so amusingly, their hopes, fears and emotions, because he knew them so well. The Empress is the only other animal he described in such detail and it seemed very unlikely that she was just a figment of his imagination.

Dates are critical in identifying Wodehouse's sources. The first mention of the Empress was in July 1927 in the short story 'Pig-Hoo-o-o-o-ey', although Wodehouse had already been struggling with early drafts of *Summer Lightning* since 1926.

Summer Lightning was the third Blandings Castle novel, but it was a very significant book in Wodehouse's career. He wrote to a friend noting that his first two Blandings novels (*Something Fresh* and *Leave it to Psmith*) dealt with the adventures of outsiders coming to Blandings. This time, he said, he wanted to write a novel based on the Threepwood family themselves. He found it very hard going, but he persevered and, late in 1928, he told his friend Bill Townend that *Summer Lightning* was finished at last. Though even then, he had to rewrite the first thirty thousand words four times.

Summer Lightning did two things. It introduced that finest of the Pink 'Uns and Pelicans, the Honourable Galahad Threepwood. It also set the pattern for every Blandings novel for the next forty-five years. Until

Summer Lightning, Lord Emsworth had many interests: gardening, protecting his yew walks, astronomy and giant pumpkins. But, from *Summer Lightning* onwards, we know that no matter what impostors or conmen may come and go, no matter what Julia, Constance or Hermione may say, the Empress is the only interest in his life. And every young suitor soon learns that the way to gain Lord Emsworth's approval is through the Empress.

In the decade 1920–30 Wodehouse was incredibly busy. He was writing and adapting plays, pouring out short stories, articles and novels at a remarkable rate. He lived at nine different addresses during those ten years and visited a dozen others, but one likely source for the Empress was obvious – Hunstanton Hall, Norfolk, the ancestral home of the Le Strange family.

Wodehouse paid his first visit in December 1924 and stayed there regularly throughout the 1920s. The owner of the Hall, Charles Le Strange, was just like Lord Emsworth, obsessed with breeding one type of animal. In his case it was Jersey cows and his cow Glenny II won the County Medal in 1929, the East Anglian championship in 1930 and the Blythwood Bowl at the National championships in 1931. Three championships in a row, just like the Empress.

For many years I was convinced that Glenny II was the model for Lord Emsworth's beloved pig. It was only in 1999 that I suddenly appreciated four factors which revealed the true source.

In the 1920s Wodehouse had a fixed daily routine. He liked to spend his mornings working, his afternoons taking a long walk, followed by a couple of hours' work in the evening. And he did not like that routine being disturbed. If he couldn't get his afternoon walk, he used to get cross and tetchy.

The second factor is that, although he liked Charles Le Strange and loved staying at Hunstanton, he disliked the social life. The County insisted on making afternoon calls, anxious to meet the famous Mr Wodehouse – and the famous Mr Wodehouse hated being met. He wanted to spend his afternoons taking a good long walk. If the County arrived, he couldn't escape.

The third factor is Wodehouse's anxiety over factual, accuracy. We know what the Empress looks like, the way her ears droop, the mild questioning expression on her face, the noise she makes when she eats, the rustle as she moves through the straw of her sty. Wodehouse would never dream of writing that from his imagination. There had to be a real pig somewhere.

The fourth factor clinched the matter. In January 1929, seven months before *Summer Lightning* came out, the *Strand* magazine published an article by Leonora Wodehouse about her stepfather. She wrote of his dislike of meeting people, his strict routine of work in the morning, how he hated to miss his long afternoon walks – and then she wrote:

> Sometimes I think of him as being amazingly faithful – I mean about places and things. An old pigsty, if he once knew the pig that lived there, is heaven to him always . . .

So there *was* a pig somewhere. I decided to look at Hunstanton more closely.

Hunstanton Hall has rolling open parkland on three sides. On the fourth side the moat has been widened to form an ornamental lake. On the far side of the lake is a belt of trees; behind the trees is a high brick wall sheltering the kitchen gardens.

The kitchen gardens are reached by a small bridge over the end of the lake leading to a path which bends out of sight in the trees. If Wodehouse wanted to avoid visitors (which he usually did) and take his regular afternoon walk (which he always did), this was the obvious route for him to take. Once through that belt of trees he was hidden from the house, and could either wander up and down the kitchen gardens or walk on to the village.

In 1986 Tom Sharpe, my wife and I visited the Hall and came through the same gap in the trees to admire the Hall across the lake. I was then still convinced that the Empress was based on Charles Le Strange's Jersey cow and it was only by chance that I noticed a small ruined structure amongst the nettles beside the kitchen-garden wall. Closer investigation (and lots of nettle stings) showed it to be an old pigsty.

This was the first spot where Wodehouse was out of sight of the house. This was where he would have paused, lit his pipe and decided where he would take his walk. And, based on everything I have read of Wodehouse and his liking for animals, I think it inconceivable that he did not establish friendly relations with the pig in residence.

So far so good, but this was over seventy years ago. Was there only one pig here? If so, was it an ordinary white pig or the black pig I was looking for?

I was then lucky enough to contact Mr Tom Mott, whose father was chauffeur at the Hall in the 1920s. Mr Mott remembers Wodehouse very well. He remembers getting a bag of sweets from him one Christmas. He remembers the punt on the lake being repainted and the name PLUM put on it because Wodehouse used it so often. He remembers the pigsty and, in answer to my last question, he confirmed what I had hoped but never really expected to hear, that in the mid-1920s the resident was a black pig!

And then, to my amazement, he mentioned that he had a photograph!

I do not claim for one moment that this was the only pig Wodehouse knew in his long life. But I have traced his movements at an average of every twelve days or so

The Empress of Blandings

between 1920 and 1930. There was certainly no pigsty at his houses in London or New York, and I have found only two visits to other country houses and then only for a few days, whereas we know Wodehouse spent nearly two months at Hunstanton in 1926, another month in 1927 and a further month in 1928. This was a pig he would have known at exactly the time he wrote 'Pig-Hoo-o-o-o-ey' and struggled with *Summer Lightning*. If ever there was a pig that gave Wodehouse the inspiration for the immortal Empress of Blandings – and there had to be an original somewhere– it was the noble animal above.

Thank heaven Mr Mott thought to photograph her all those years ago.

N. T. P. MURPHY